Extraordinary

Extraordinary

DAVID GILMOUR

PATRICK CREAN EDITIONS
HarperCollins*PublishersLtd*

HarperCollins Publishers Ltd
2 Bloor Street East, 20th Floor
Toronto, Ontario, Canada
M4W 1A8

www.harpercollins.ca

Library and Archives Canada Cataloguing in Publication
information is available upon request

ISBN 978-1-44342-370-0

Printed and bound in the United States of America
RRD 9 8 7 6 5 4 3 2 1

For Stephanie Saunders

For as the dead exist only in ourselves, it is ourselves that we strike without ceasing when we persist in recalling the blows we have dealt them.

—MARCEL PROUST

Extraordinary

One

WHAT? YOU DIDN'T KNOW I HAD A SISTER?
Yes, Sally, a half-sister really. She was fifteen
years older than me, my mother's daughter from
a turbulent first marriage. I saw her now and
again when I was growing up, but probably the
difference in our ages, a generation, and the fact
that she never lived with us, made her seem more
like a sympathetic aunt. She swatted me once,
just an impatient cuff on the back of the head,
when I was eight or nine—I'd knocked over a
flower jar in her kitchen—and I thought, You
can't do that, you're not my mother. And yet it
wasn't quite like a quarrel with my brother, not
on the same level, so to speak, as with a peer.
How you feel about someone when you're very

young, their stature in the world compared with yours, sometimes never changes. Which made certain moments between Sally and me confusing. Especially later on.

By the time I was conscious enough to wonder why things were the way they were, she was already married. How such a lovely creature (long face, dark hair) ended up with a blockhead like Bruce Sanders, I'll never understand. But I suppose that's the nature of people, even family: you never really get to know anyone that well, even when they try to explain themselves.

Anyway. For sixteen years, she endured sulks, punishing silences and God knows what kind of lonely moments, until one night she didn't; and the next day, Bruce Sanders woke up in the guest room of his own house, the evening's final words thudding between his small ears: "I'm leaving you."

It may have taken her a while to get there, but when she did, my goodness, she acted with

the efficiency of a guillotine. The straightest
line between two points. I was only a teenager,
but it felt as though I had just had my first
glimpse into affairs of the heart: when a woman's finished with you, she's really finished.

With Chloe, her twelve-year-old daughter,
in tow (her son stayed at home with Bruce),
she took a studio apartment in San Miguel de
Allende, a sun-baked town in the mountains
north of Mexico City, and resumed her career
as a painter—something for which she was
gifted but the execution of which had been
discouraged by a husband who thought the
whole business "unrealistic." A few weeks
later, Sally attended an afternoon cocktail
party at a house on the Callejón de los
Muertos, tripped on the carpet, smacked her
head against the fireplace and broke her neck.
Returning to Toronto on a gurney, she spent
six months in rehab and the rest of her life
in a wheelchair.

Nice deal, eh? But she was a hearty soul, and even with the wheelchair, the crutches, the falling down here and there, she raised her preteen daughter all but single-handedly. Her ex-husband, Bruce, in a state of ill-disguised pleasure at the hand life had dealt her, said, "Move back in with me," the implication being, Now that you're not in the game anymore, now that no one *else* will take you, you might as well come back.

But no handouts, thank you. Sally and Chloe found a way to live and be happy. As for me, I wasn't around much, to say the least. Sometimes I'd go up to her apartment in the northern part of the city and drink too much and get her to drink too much and then leave for another year or two. The truth is, I was so distracted with the failure of my own life that it felt as though I didn't have the time to go out of my way, even momentarily, for anyone else. Although God knows what I was doing instead.

Still, it makes me queasy with regret, even after all these years, to think about it. Because I loved her, I really did. But I was under the assumption that she would always be there, this not-quite-mother, not-quite-sister, that there was no need to tend to it, to look after it like a garden. And then, suddenly, it was too late by years. Simply too late.

Looking back on things, I suppose it's the reason I did what I did that night, to make up for all those times I glanced toward the top of the city and said fuck it and went about my own business instead.

Do the dead forgive us? I wonder. I hope so. But I suspect not. I suspect they do nothing at all, like a spark flying from a burning campfire: they just go *psssst* and that's it. How they felt about you in that last second is where you remain, at least in *your* thoughts, for eternity. Or rather, until you go *psssst* too.

Years went by. Chloe graduated from high school with green hair and a dagger tattoo on her right arm, went to university in Montreal and then left town to do a graduate degree in the States. Several months later, Sally telephoned me out of the blue one night and asked me to come over to her apartment. To bring a bottle of Russian vodka.

By the end of the evening, I'd agreed to help her kill herself.

Over the next five weeks, I raided second-floor medicine cabinets at dinners and parties until I found what I was looking for in the attic of a sweet but doddery aunt. I don't need to mention the name of the drug here. It was a sleeping pill yanked off the market only a few months after its appearance. Quite the scandal. You mixed it with a couple of stiff belts before bed and you didn't get up in the morning. End of story. Yours anyway.

So one June evening, I climbed the eighteen flights of stairs that ran up the back of her apartment building, hurried along the flowered carpeting in the hallway and let myself in. It was important that no one see me.

Candles were burning. I could see she had made herself up a bit, had on a green silk dressing gown.

"I had a nap this afternoon. I'm as fresh as a daisy," she said.

I said, "You look wonderful tonight." I went into the kitchen, cracked open the ice tray, made a brace of burnt martinis, poured a round into two tulip glasses and sat down beside her.

Taking the glass in her hand, partly crabbed, she said, "Cheers."

"Cheers indeed."

We talked about all sorts of things—the city's mayor, a stolen Cézanne that had recently turned

up in a Chicago attic, mentholated cigarettes, the
Dave Brubeck Quartet, Marlon Brando, the arrest
of Klaus Barbie, the final episode of *M.A.S.H.* I
didn't mention the pills, nor the purpose of the
evening; neither did she. It was, for a while there,
like a Saturday night between two old friends, a
forty-nine-year-old woman and her thirty-four-
year-old brother. Half-brother, I know, but you
wouldn't have guessed it that night.

"Let's put on some music," she said, and I
did, a collection of snazzy Mexican folk songs,
which, I don't know why, reminded me of an
incident that had happened years before; how,
when I was fourteen, in secret and against the
wishes of my parents, she had smuggled me
out of the house and driven me to see a girl at
a small-town dance fifty miles away, returning hours later to fetch me. (The girl being, in
the parlance of my mother, "a cunning little
tramp.") It may sound like a small thing for Sally
to have done, this drive down a dark country

highway, but I was so hungry for that young girl, for her small face and for the mysterious smell that lay under her jeans, that it was—or seemed to be at the moment—a matter of life and death. And Sally, as though she had maintained one foot still in childhood, understood the *degree* of it. The urgency of it. It took me years to put words to it, but I intuited something crucial that night: that the doing of something you don't need to do for someone whose approval you don't need is an extraordinarily reliable test of character. As the years have gone by—I recently celebrated my fifty-eighth birthday—I think more and more that the course of one's life and the loyalties which colour it are the flowers that have grown in such unnoticed gardens.

"Did I ever tell you how kind that was?" I said suddenly.

Sally appeared to think about that, her glass tilting at a dangerous angle on her lap. "You were in love," she said simply.

"I was. But all that *driving*."

She took a sip from her glass. "I like these martinis. How do you make them again?"

I must have looked surprised as one is sometimes at the end of a Chekhov short story. You don't know what it means or what it implies about life, but you know it's the truth. Sally would never live to make a burnt martini, but she wanted to know how to do it anyway.

In the seconds that followed, I felt a swoosh—a sudden, terrible regret. She seemed to read my thoughts, because she said, "You were fine."

I worried I was going to burst into tears and lure the focus of the evening onto myself.

"I haven't been much of a brother," I said.

She responded with an absolving laugh. "You're making up for it now. You gave me this," she said, and raised her martini glass in bent fingers. "But you're hesitating. You haven't changed your mind?"

"No, don't worry about that."

"Good. I don't want to worry about that."

"You don't have to," I said.

"Just think of it as returning the favour for driving you to the dance."

I didn't know how to take this, whether to let it alone or not. Was it a joke? Of course it was, this retreat into flippancy. And yet not a joke you could feel good laughing about. I didn't know quite where to rest my eyes. But I thought, Don't perform. Just look at her. But I have never been good with silence, it makes my heart crash, and in that moment it seemed as though she too could hear it thumping and again came to my rescue. "Whatever happened to that girl?"

"She met someone else."

"Ah," Sally said, not surprised but not superior to it either. A tone of voice that summed you up like a sudden, flattering glance in a store window.

"Apparently, he was a very good dancer," I said.

"They always are, those summer boys."

"Anyway, I got over it."

"You did indeed."

I waited for the small blossom of pleasure to recede and then, seeking a fresher, more subtle kind, added, "Between you and me, Sally, I've always talked a bigger game than I played."

We fell silent for a moment.

"Were you?" I said.

"Was I what?"

"A good dancer."

"Oh, I loved dancing. I'd dance with *anyone*." She glanced out the window and I could see her as a teenager, at a dance, in a tangle of young bodies and coloured lights and those neon things they used to stamp your hand with, and for a second I wondered whatever had happened to all those bodies, those *young* bodies; and again it struck me that life was such a harsh business that no one, not even the beautiful like Sally, was ever safe.

I said, "Would you like another martini?"

"Oh boy, would I ever."

I went into the kitchen, the pills still in my pocket. I had put a ball of cotton batten in the plastic vial so they wouldn't rattle when I moved. It was a clean white kitchen with a lot of room. It was the kitchen of a woman who had raised children, who liked order in her life.

"Don't forget the Scotch," she said.

"It's already in."

When I came back, one of the candles was sputtering. I blew it out, found a pair of scissors in the desk drawer, cut the wick down and relit it. Settled back in my chair, I noticed that Sally's eyes, pools of ink in a slightly swollen face, were observing me with what, I'm not sure. It was the regard of someone who is seeing something *behind* their eyes. I couldn't tell, though, if it was good or bad.

I said, "Can I ask you something, Sally?"

"Yes."

"I was wondering about your marriage the other day."

She nodded her head as if to a question she had been asked many times before. "What part of the marriage?" she asked neutrally.

"The *why* part."

Again she nodded, this time with a hint of amused sleepiness. "I had my eye on someone else. To say the least. But I couldn't get him. Or *keep* him, anyway."

"Tell me."

I could see her recede into herself and then re-emerge. She had found something in there that pleased her. "There was a boy who went to my high school, a narrow-hipped cowboy. No, he really *was* a cowboy—wore a narrow-brimmed hat, drove a pickup truck, listened to country and western music."

"A cowboy hat?"

"Even to school. He knew the etiquette, when you could wear a hat and when you had to take it off. Like when you go in a building, you take your hat off, but when you sit at a counter in a diner, you can leave it on. Some smart aleck stopped him in the corridor once, a hockey player, and said in a big attention-getting voice, 'Hey Tex, can I try on your hat?' He said, 'Sure, if I can try on your underwear.'"

"Wow."

"He made furniture. Kitchen tables, chairs, headboards. I remember once he was in such a rush to finish and get over to my place that he had wood chips in his eyebrows. *God*, he smelt good. You know what the French say about smell?"

"I do, yes."

"Even in the truck I could smell him. He had a narrow chest and he always wore a cowboy shirt. It would have looked corny on anyone else, those imitation pearl buttons, but on him,

it was like he was born into it. Like a skin. He
called me Miss. He'd say, 'What time do you
want me to come and get you, Miss?' or, 'We
should be getting you home pretty soon, Miss.'
His name was Terry Blanchard."

"Did you ever kiss him?"

"Every chance I got."

"And?"

"Ever kissed a cowboy?"

I said, "So what happened to him?"

"He had some kind of trouble in town. One
night he turned up outside my window. He
knocked on the glass and said he was going away
for a while but he'd write. Would I write him
back? And then he kissed me. There was a big
country moon that night, the kind you can reach
out with your finger and almost touch. I could
see it over his shoulder. I said, 'Come into my
bed.' It just came out, like hearing yourself talk
in a dream.

"He slipped over the window ledge back-

wards and fell onto the bed, his boots in the air.
You could see them against the skyline.

"I heard my grandmother walk by my room.
She said, 'Everything okay in there, Sally?' She
must have seen his truck in the driveway. And
I said, 'Grandma, just fine. I'm going to sleep
now.' Those country people, they're a lot more
sophisticated than you'd think. I never asked her
and she never asked me, but every so often I'd
catch her staring at me. Everybody gets up to
something private, it's just that every generation
thinks they're the first ones to do it right."

"So did he write?"

"Never. Not a word. I used to go out to the
mailbox—it was at the end of a long driveway—
and throw stones at the power lines and the
crows, even at the mailbox itself, while I was
waiting. An old guy and his son delivered the
mail in a car. I'd see the car at the far end of the
highway where it broke through the cornfields.
Walter, the son, would be in the passenger seat,

his tanned arm hanging out the window with the mail in his hand. They'd slow down and I'd grab the mail. I think Walter had a tiny thing for me, but he had a kind of funny-shaped head, like a paint can. I suppose I was cruelly uninterested in him. I'd just snatch the mail, and without even saying goodbye I'd start to go through it—the local newspaper, ads for baking sales, bills from the local hardware store, even Christmas cards that had gotten lost for six months. I'd start off full of hope, there'd be all this stuff, but then there'd be five letters left, then three, then none, and I'd go through the pile again as though maybe I'd missed it.

"But never a letter. Once, I even waved down the car as it pulled away. 'Are you sure there's nothing for me?' The father said, 'Well, let's take another look.' And he did. 'Maybe tomorrow, Sally,' he said.

"It was the longest walk back to the house— a hot day, cicadas roaring, those big pointless fields and nothing to look forward to. I let the screen door bang behind me. My grandmother said, 'Sally, don't let that door bang, it scares the willies out of me.'

"I went back into my bedroom and lay down on the bed, the wallpaper with little wooden rocking chairs on it, the yellow fields outside. I thought, I've got to *do* something, read a book or write in my diary or play some records, and I kept thinking my way through it: open up the record box, take out a forty-five, put it on the record player and start it up. But it just seemed like too much work. Everything did. Everything seemed *exhausting*. I just lay there till supper.

"I never found out what the trouble was. He just vanished."

"And your mother? Where was your mother, *our* mother, while all this was going on?"

"She was around. At her convenience, of course. Sometimes she'd come by in a grey car with a big grille with flies stuck in it and take me to the Tastee Freeze in town for a hamburger—it was a ritual we had—and then she'd take me for a long drive on backcountry roads, let me light her cigarettes for her. She was a great talker. A good listener too, to be fair—as long as you said what she wanted to hear.

"On one of these drives, just as it was getting dark and we were heading back to my grandfather's, I told her about Terry Blanchard, about that night he tumbled into my bed. It wasn't a confession, it was just that talking about it was as close as I could get to doing it again."

"And what did she say?"

"She asked me if I felt better now that I'd talked about it. And I said yes. And then she said something that I have never forgotten. She said, 'You're going to feel good about all this for a while and then later, when I'm gone and you're alone again and the excitement of talking about it has worn off, you're going to go back to feeling the way you did before. And that's normal.

Just remember that that's normal. There's nothing wrong with you.' Then she told me about going out on a date with a Hollywood movie star when she was just nineteen."

"Who was it?"

"I think it was Errol Flynn. She claimed to not know this from personal experience, but someone had told her his dink was so big he had to strap it to his leg. It made me laugh. A funny story to hear from your mother. But I don't know. You could never be sure with her. She told me she wrote a short story for the *New Yorker* once, too. But I never saw it. Maybe she did. But I doubt it."

"The *New Yorker*? That's a pretty tall order."

"It certainly is."

"And was she right?" I asked.

"About what?"

"About how you were going to feel later."

"She was. After she left, I kept looking at the clock. An hour later, I was still fine, happy even. Two hours later, same thing. But then later, after dinner, I was watching television with my grandfather, and I could feel things starting to darken again. It was as if some kind of poison was slowly creeping into my body, like some awful *leak*, and the whole good feeling I'd had with my mother just slipped away. I couldn't concentrate on the TV show, it was like the screen was a sort of anchor that allowed my thoughts to go in some very gloomy directions. I was afraid it would show on my face or that my grandfather would hear it in my responses. He liked to talk during television shows, but that night it was driving me crazy, as though I had something important to figure out and he was interrupting me from it with his chatter.

"So I went to bed. But here's something odd. Sometime near morning, it was just getting light, I found myself on the floor. I was soaked in sweat, I was menstruating, I thought I was dying. Dying of a broken heart. But

then I thought about Terry Blanchard, about
that night he came tumbling into my bed, and
I didn't feel anything. And then, like sticking
your hand in a basin of hot water to test it, I
thought about him again. Nothing. I mean,
absolutely nothing. Gone. I thought, I'm free
of him! This is how you do it, this is how you
recover from love. And little by little, I started
to notice things in the world—a snowbank, a
name written on the washroom wall—without
all of it leading back to him.

"It must have been the next summer—I was
seventeen—when a beat-up white car pulled
into the driveway and a man with small ears
and an acne-scarred complexion shambled up
to the house. He was lost, he said. Was there an
asbestos factory near here? He was late for a
pickup. Could he use the phone? It was Bruce
Sanders. Eight months later, I married him."

"Eight months?"

"The details don't matter. Not now, not

at this stage. But he was a great lover. A mind
reader. You're surprised?"

"Why, yes. Yes, I am." A childhood memory
of Bruce slouching through our living room at a
Christmas party turned over in my memory like
a playing card.

"So was I," she said, her eyebrows poised
on a deadpan face. In that moment, in that light,
she looked Asian. "Anyway," Sally said, "I'm
through with that stuff. I have been for a while.
It all seems just so messy."

I wasn't sure how to answer and looked into
my glass. A car honked three times eighteen
floors down. I heard a jet passing over. "I didn't
know we were so close to the airport," I said.

Picking up on my discomfort, and probably sorry she'd thrown that in, Sally went on.
"Bruce Sanders was certainly nothing to look
at, on the surface anyway. He wore a kind of
military brush cut that stuck up like a raccoon's
pelt. But he had a wiry little body with deep tan

lines from working outside. He was very strong, deceptively so. There was a lot of dangerous leverage in those arms. I saw him lay his forearm across the throat of some local lacrosse hero one night and lift him up the wall, right off the ground.

"There was something about Bruce I admired, some old-fashioned, tight-lipped masculinity. They are a rare thing these days, real men. Too many sissies eager to get on the right side of women." Pause. "What women like about men is that they're *not* women. And they don't think like women."

"We're simple creatures," I said, and we both laughed. We were having a preposterous time. I caught myself thinking, Should we be doing this? Or should we be doing something else? We are talking about what we're talking about because that's what she wants to talk about. But is this really going to happen? Now that we're here? Is she waiting for me to say

stop, or am I waiting for her? Is this going to
happen because we're both waiting for the other
to say something? And if I were to say something, what would it be? What would I *mean*? If
I were in her place, what would *I* want?

"Sally . . ." I began, but her hand fluttered
me to silence. I had not considered this part, at
least not the way it now presented itself.

She went on: "That said, Bruce was not very
socially *able*. Sulked in public gatherings. I think
he felt out of his intellectual league if the conversation ever steered toward movies or even the
Beatles. For some reason, he found them especially infuriating."

"The Beatles?"

"He said the only reason they get to be
the Beatles is that other people don't get to
be. Whatever the hell that means. Anyway, it
annoyed him when I talked too much at parties.
When I got excited. Excited because I was so
hungry for talk that I'd drink too much some-

times and get very, very talkative. He'd sulk for days afterwards. That was my punishment.

"Anyway, I married him. I looked out my bedroom window one afternoon and saw all those flat fields and thought, Why not? We had a wedding in a small country church with a graveyard you could see from the pews. Afterwards, we went to a party in town. You know why? Because someone told me they'd seen Terry Blanchard outside the hardware store and that maybe he'd be there. Isn't that pathetic? God, what was I thinking? Going to a party on my wedding night because this other guy might be there! And here I'd thought I was over him."

"Was he there?"

"No, thank God. I couldn't relax until I was sure. I kept peeking at the door every time someone came in. I suppose that's how you know you're with the wrong person—when you keep looking to see who's coming in the door. It wasn't a bad party, if you were drunk enough. Which I was."

"And did things get better?"

"Your body always tells you where you belong—and where you don't. Sometimes when I was having Sunday dinner with Bruce's parents, who were perfectly decent people, by the way, salt-of-the-earth types, I'd feel this sensation in my body, a sensation that said simply, *You don't belong here, these are not your people.*"

"Did you ever find your people?"

"Yes, I did."

"Who?"

"You. Among other people."

After a pause, I said, "Tell me you had a good life, Sally."

"I was lucky in a lot of ways. I just used up my luck early. But yes, I had a good life."

"With happy moments?"

"Many," she said easily. "Everyone does."

"Tell me one."

"Leaving my husband. I enjoyed that."

"Was it precipitous or gradual?" I said.

"What do you mean?"

"Your decision to leave. It took a long time."

"Years. Are you sure you're interested in this?"

"Very."

"There's something numbing about disap-
pointment. You have to act on it quickly or time
begins to gallop," she said.

"You'd like Chekhov," I said.

"Can you put a cube of ice in this? But no
more vodka. I'll be up peeing all night."

"How are your legs?"

"The same. But only at night."

I came back in from the kitchen.

"Will you turn the light out in there?" she said.

I went back and did it.

"Where was I?" She had slipped off to other
thoughts. "Oh yes. By now I had two kids,
Chloe and Kyle. We had a narrow little house in
Toronto. Nice place. I did the interior myself.

It was my birthday, I was thirty-three. Yes, yes, I know what you're going to say: the age that Christ was crucified. I didn't see things quite so grandly. Although it turned out to be a big year indeed. The kids were old enough to look after themselves, and that night Bruce took me to an Italian restaurant, a new place I'd read about in a magazine.

"Our table wasn't ready, so they sat us in the bar. We had a martini and looked out over the restaurant, all the people eating in this lovely copper light, and suddenly, I could barely believe my eyes, there, facing me, sitting not ten feet away, was Terry Blanchard. I'd heard he was in the Middle East working for an oil company. But no, there he was. He was sitting with a thick-bodied woman, the sort of woman whose nylons you can hear cracking when she walks across the room. Confident. Talking. Terry listening. And I thought, He cannot love her."

"How'd he look?"

"Wonderful. Those men age so well. He was snappily done up, a tie, white shirt. And I had the ridiculous, ever-so-quick thought that somehow he had known he was going to see me and had gotten, you know, *dolled up* for it. Does your generation use that word, 'dolled up'?"

"Not really. But I know what you mean."

"Anyway, I know it's nonsense, but that's what I thought. Meanwhile, I could hear Bruce chewing on his olive and breathing through his nose."

"Did you say anything?"

"No. I just kept taking these little mouse-peeks at him. And I think he was doing the same to me, but we never did it at the same time."

"Why didn't you go over?"

"Too shy."

"Too shy?"

"No, that's not true. The fact is, I didn't feel especially pretty. I felt like I'd put on weight,

that there was something clumsy about how I
looked, and that he'd be disappointed. But I
wanted *him* to come over. I could feel the skin on
my face go very tight, like I was sitting in a high
wind. It was awful. But sort of wild, too."

"And?"

"It was astonishing how much I remembered
about him—his shirt, his underarms, even the
wood dust in his eyebrows. I was surprised that
it was all so vivid, so immediate. So *yesterday*. He
had remained frozen in my heart exactly as I had
felt about him the last time I saw him."

"Did it make you sad?"

"It didn't. It made me feel sort of light-
headed and exhilarated. I can't imagine why. But
I wanted to tell someone. I wished I was with
someone other than Bruce so I could whisper,
'You see that man over there . . . ' And then tell
them the story."

"Then what happened?"

"Then he was gone. The table was empty.

Napkins on the tablecloth, water glasses half
empty, the waiter clearing away stuff. To this
day, I don't know how I missed him leaving."

"And did you see him again?"

"I went back to the restaurant a few times.
Alone. I sat at the copper bar. But I never saw
him. Still, I've always been curious, always
wanted to ask him, 'What were you thinking when
you saw me, what were you remembering?'"

"Oh dear."

"Well, yes and no. Because of what happened later. Just a few weeks later. I'm not sure
it would have happened if I hadn't spotted Terry
Blanchard in a restaurant on the night of my
thirty-third birthday." After a moment's reflec-
tion, she continued: "We'd been invited to a
cocktail party in Forest Hill. I can't remember
who invited us. But it was a splashy affair. Not
really our crowd. I was excited about going. I've
always liked getting out and about."

Out and about. Very Sally, that phrase.

She went on: "There were quite a few men there, and I was getting a good deal of attention, which often happened. I'm not bragging. I was a good-looking woman."

"You still are."

She paused with a hint of relish to collect her thoughts. "I was having a chat in the corner with a man I had met that evening. Marek Grunbaum was his name. Handsome in an Eastern European, sort of state-police way. The kind of face that knocks at your door at three in the morning and your wife never sees you again. But he wasn't like that at all. Tough, yes—he owned a factory that made car parts. It was clear from the ring on my finger that I was married, but it was also apparent that that didn't concern him very much.

"He had a beautiful pink handkerchief in the breast pocket of his jacket, and such elegant manners, the capacity to suggest that everyone in the room was worthy of attention but that you somehow were *more* worthy. A party trick, maybe, but hard to resist, nevertheless. Who *isn't* stirred by absolute attention?

"I noticed him discreetly glance around the room. What was he looking for? Did he have a jealous wife? Then I realized what it was."

"What was it?"

"He wanted to see what my husband *looked* like. But he was confused, because, looking over the crowd, there was no one who appeared to look like the kind of person I would be married to. You could see his eyes move over the English husband of the hostess, then over a local politician, then a retired hockey player who was very much *à la vogue* in that circle. They like to adopt people, those Forest Hill folk, athletes, ex-convicts, priests, writers—creatures of a different cloth. It lasts a while and then the circle closes again. Anyway, Marek didn't stop, not for a second, on Bruce, who was wearing a green shirt and leaning with one arm on the fireplace mantel, his jacket open, his little pot belly exposed. Leaning and giving me the look. Eyes half shut like a reptile. I could feel myself getting nervous. I was thinking, Oh-oh, he's mad at me. He's going to sulk in the car, he's going to get out of bed in the morning and sit on the couch in his pyjama bottoms, smoking a cigarette and clearing his throat. *No, nope, nothing's wrong.* And I'd flounce around, chirping like a bird, trying to cajole him out of his foul mood. God, is there anything that creates self-disgust faster than apologizing when you haven't done anything wrong? The person you end up hating is yourself.

"So I waved him over. I thought it would make everything transparent, innocent. I introduced them. 'Marek, this is my husband.' Marek asked him a few questions. Just good manners. Did he work in the neighbourhood, how long had he lived in Toronto, how old were our children? But the ball never came back over the net.

Bruce stood there, drink in hand, yes, no, looking into the contents of the glass as if he were
waiting for the ice to melt.

"It worked. He'd done it before. He knew
how to do it, this bubble of toxicity. It drove
Marek away. Within seconds, everything was
gone. Marek took everything with him when he
walked away. There was just me left behind—
me and this red-faced man with his sports jacket
riding up at the back.

"I peeked over his shoulder, hoping Marek
might be looking this way or waiting to come
back. But no—he had landed in a clutter of
middle-aged women, tennis players, rich, pol-
ished, tactile. He was theirs now."

"And then?"

"We went home a little while later, Bruce
and I. But something miraculous happened in
the car. It was as if a virus had come of age. I
didn't formulate the sentence, I didn't think of
its ramifications. But it found its way out of my

mouth all on its own. I said, 'I don't love you anymore.'

"We drove the rest of the way in silence. I went into the house and straight to the kitchen. When he came in after me, I pulled a steak knife out of the drawer. I didn't say anything, I just turned around and stood there with a steak knife in my hand. And that was the end of it."

A small bell pinged and the elevator doors clanged shut at the end of the corridor.

"Tell me if I'm talking too much," she said.

"Go on. Please."

"I moved my children into a yellow apartment and got a job in an art gallery. A boutique in Yorkville next door to a French bistro. To have somewhere to go every day, people to say hello to—those wonderful, sparkly, frivolous conversations about nothing at all—to have my own paycheque. It was the happiest I'd been in years, maybe my whole adult life. And no one to make me nervous."

"And Marek?"

"Ah, Marek," she said, settling back into her chair. "I don't believe in God, but if I did, I'd say that the arrival of Marek Grunbaum with his pink handkerchief that night was God saying to me, 'I've overlooked you. Here's a make-up present.' He had a wife and three children who adored him. He made a few awkward sounds about leaving his wife, but we both knew he wasn't going to, that I was the latest in a short but piquant list of lovers. That was fine. Just knowing that every Tuesday night I was going to go to that bistro, sit at the same table, *our* table, have two ice-cold martinis and a bottle of wine, and then go home and get laid—just having *that* to look forward to made the whole week divine. I hope that doesn't sound coarse."

"No. Not at all."

"There were two gay men living downstairs. Sean and his boyfriend, Peter. They worried about me: was I lonely? was I unhappy seeing a

married man? did I have enough money? Isn't
that a scream? The only time in my life I *didn't*
need to be worried about. It was as if a grey
screen between me and the world had been lifted
and I could see everything so vividly.

"One day, I'd just finished reupholstering a
chesterfield—Sean had passed it along—and I
found myself with a couple of bolts of cloth left
over. Just for fun, while I was watching television, I took a pair of long scissors and cut out the
shape of a sailboat, a blue sailboat, and pasted
it onto a square of leftover yellow cloth. I put a
mast on it and a sun and a big swordfish jumping
in the air. Then I hung it over the fireplace.

"Peter Ungster, my neighbour, came upstairs
one evening to borrow a corkscrew and noticed
the wall hanging. He lingered in front of it with
a sort of puzzled expression on his face. 'Where
did you get *that*?' he said. (He sounded a bit like
Truman Capote when he talked, like a sleepy
porpoise. How he survived growing up in a min-

ing town in northern Ontario is a mystery. But
that's another story.) 'Is it for *sale*?' he asked,
tilting his head. I thought he was playing it up a
bit, indulging the new widow in her little hobby,
but he wrote me a cheque for twenty-five dollars
and took the swordfish back home with him. You
never forget a moment like that, the first time
you sell something you made. The money makes
it different, makes *you* different.

"His boyfriend, Sean, knew a woman who
owned a shop for children's things: toys, pictures, puppets, stuffed animals. She saw the
sailboat and ordered five of them in different
colours. A red sailboat, a green sailboat. I put
a moon overhead, a flying fish sailing over the
bow, a lantern on the mast. Soon I had two teenage girls working for me, doing the cutting, the
dyeing, the shipping. I kept one as a souvenir.
It's faded a bit—the sun coming through the
window does that—but it's over there. Yes,
that's it, over the sideboard."

A blue whale winked mischievously at me from the mouth of a lagoon.

"And the job at the art gallery?"

She leaned forward in a gust of enthusiasm. "It was a period in my life where I couldn't seem to do anything wrong. Things just fell into place, like musical notes. Most people who work in the art world don't wish you well, especially if you're leaving to do something artistic. They want you to fail—it makes their lives less haunting. I understand that, and I expected it. Long faces, sour faces. But I guess life had just given me enough shit for the time being. They threw me a party at the boutique. A little one. Marek Grunbaum came in a cream suit. He looked smashing. A fluffed pink handkerchief stuffed in his breast pocket. It was like showing off your boyfriend at a high school dance. He drove me home that night, and I remember looking out the car window as we passed up through the city, past the parliament buildings, past that park with the man on the horse, and I remember thinking, I'll never be this happy again."

"Were you?"

"Was I what?"

"Ever that happy again?"

"Of course I was. You're never just happy *once* in your life. Life isn't like that." She paused. "Will you have a small Drambuie with me? It's up there in the cupboard over the fridge. Yes, there, right behind your hand. Could you heat it up? Just put it in those snifters and pop it into the microwave."

"Did Marek like Drambuie?"

Deadpan. Eyebrows raised. "Marek liked everything. It's wonderful to be with a man who adores a woman's body. Every inch of it. But wait." She pointed to the microwave. "Yes. Thirty seconds should be enough."

"Is that too hot?"

"No, it's perfect. Smell that. I've been saving this for a rainy day."

I sat back down. It was eleven o'clock.

"My little sailboats caught on. I did a craft show in Memphis. A rep from a middle-sized American chain saw my stuff and bought me out. I like that about Americans, how they do business. They come in, they look around, and they write a cheque. No pussyfooting. So suddenly there I was, with a bunch of money and two teenage children. What to do?

"Peter Ungster was trying on a new hat in my mirror, and he said in that funny voice, 'Why don't you move to *Mex*ico? There's an artists' colony in San Miguel de Allende. That sounds like baloney, I know, and there *is* a lot of baloney down there, but not entirely. You could open a little shop—you could paint—do whatever you want. Leonard Cohen lives there. Or people *say* he lives there. Nobody ever seems to *see* him. For a while I had a friend there, an antique collector, *soi-disant*, but it turned out he was just looking for some Mexican boy to fuck him in the bum and leave him for dead. Which isn't far from what happened. But don't get me get started on that one.'

"So I went. San Miguel is a pretty town nine thousand feet up in the air with a sweeping cathedral right in the centre. Somebody in the Cucaracha bar told me it was designed entirely from a single European postcard. But people start drinking early in those towns and they kind of make stuff up. One moment it's not true, next moment it is. No one seems to care.

"I took Chloe with me. She was twelve years old. I couldn't leave her with Bruce. That would have been like leaving her in a black-and-white television show. Besides, she wanted to go. She was very adventurous. She could hardly wait."

"What did Bruce say?"

"He threatened to take me to court. But I called his bluff. I wasn't rattled by him anymore. I said, 'Okay, Bruce, I'll leave her up here with you.' That scared the shit out of him. He wasn't a mean spirit, he just didn't want me to have my cake and eat it too. As if you'd do anything else with your cake *except* eat it. But the notion of a gangly, phone-hogging, incessantly hungry, expensive, operatic teenage girl running up and down the stairs with a pair of school friends really shook him up."

"So he folded?"

"Like a deck chair. In fact, he *gave* me money. He pretended it was for Chloe's expenses, but I think it was to make sure she actually *went*."

"And her brother, Kyle? Can I ask what happened there?"

Her face clouded. "You know that story," she said softly. "I made a mistake. I was so hungry to be happy that I made a mistake." She looked toward the window.

I said, "We don't have—" but she went on.

"Kyle was seventeen. He wanted to stay with his friends. Besides, I didn't want to strip Bruce of everything. I worried he'd kill himself. But I should have tried harder, I should have insisted."

I could see her sinking into a fog of distress. I said, "Did he know about Marek?"

Sally had disappeared on me, but then returned. "Who? Kyle?"

"No, Bruce."

"I made it clear not to wait around. It was a kindness, really. He was mooning around my yellow apartment one evening, waiting for Chloe to collect her clothes for a sleepover. I sat him down in the kitchen, I put a Scotch in his hand, and I said, 'There's something I want you to understand. Even if this thing with Marek Grunbaum doesn't work out, even if it doesn't work out with the man *after* him, I will never, under any circumstances, come back to you.'"

"Jesus."

"He needed to hear it. Bruce was one of those men, you know the kind: A woman leaves them and they take on a look of wounded confusion, as if the whole thing is a kind of *problème psychi-atrique*. A fit of madness that could, conceivably, vanish as quickly as it came on. You know how it goes: *My wife went nuts, but I'm being patient.* They overlook the fact that you've hated them for years. They overlook the fact that you've got a new boyfriend, lost twenty pounds, wear different clothes and have an expensive new haircut."

"Did he believe you?"

"He looked at me with those half-closed eyes and said, 'I'm not in any hurry.' At which point I snapped at him. I regret it. Sort of. No, I don't. I said, 'For God's sake, Bruce, you can't jerk off for the rest of your life!'

"Chloe and I flew to Mexico City and then took a bus for a couple of hundred miles north through the desert and up into the mountains. A friend of Peter's, Freddie Steigman, met us at the bus station. He was a native New Yorker, a pensioner, thirty-five years with Allstate Insurance. He used to be roommates with Edward Albee.

Back when they were in their twenties. Albee was a poet then, apparently a very bad one. You know him?"

"The *Who's Afraid of Virginia Woolf?* guy."

"Yeah, that's him. When he retired, Freddie came to San Miguel for a holiday. But he fell in love with the Mexican boy who looked after the hotel swimming pool. The boy disappeared after a couple of weeks, but Freddie stayed on."

The candle sputtered. Sally watched it for a moment, her eyes sleepy. Getting ready to leave the party.

"What was Albee like?" I asked.

Two

SHE LOOKED UP FROM THE CANDLE FLAME.
"Are we going to do this thing?"

"Yes."

"And you'll stay?"

"Of course I'll stay."

And I thought, Nothing works out the way
you think it will. And this won't either. So I
know which way it won't work out. But the
other way, the way it will, that I don't know.
How was it supposed to go again? The climb up
eighteen flights of stairs, the quick walk down
the hall, into the apartment. But then what? I
can't seem to recall. What did I think would
come *after* the apartment? The next day, the
next week. A year later. Five years later. Surely

I must have thought about that: that the end of
something isn't necessarily the end of it. A man
parts the curtains one morning and discovers an
entire *planet* revolving just outside the window.
Oh, I *see.*

Sally looked back at the flame, nodding.
"What were we talking about?"

"Edward Albee."

"Somebody asked Freddie about him
one night when he was holding court in the
Cucaracha bar. 'If homosexuality had not
existed, Albee would have invented it,' Freddie
said." Sally smiled affectionately. "You could tell
he'd said it before. Please, another Drambuie."

In the kitchen doorway, I turned around. "I
have to turn the light on now. Close your eyes."

Settled with a brandy snifter that burned like
dark gold in her hand, she continued. "Freddie

Steigman dressed like a slightly down-at-the-
heels salesman from the fifties. Heavy New York
accent. A face part bulldog, part baseball mitt.
Loved to drink. He wore a baby blue linen jacket
every day of the year. He had two or three of
them, identically wrinkled, and a white Mexican
shirt that he kept unbuttoned almost to the waist.
He reminded me of the retired history teacher in
The Catcher in the Rye. Except it was endearing,
it was tender, it was adorable, this old blade with
a bony chest insisting he was still in the game.

"And he *was*. Once a month, Freddie took
the bus to Mexico City, hired the prettiest boy he
could find in the red light district. He paid well,
never got beaten up and came back the following
Monday with a light step and interested in everything. I *adored* him.

"Freddie knew everybody in San Miguel,
and he liked knowing everyone. He got me a
ground floor sublet, with an old piano somebody had left behind, a patio and a view of the

mountains. When someone asked me where I lived, I'd say, 'Callejón de los Muertos.' The Street of Dead Lanterns. I loved how it rolled off my tongue. Three weeks after my arrival, Freddie threw a party for me.

"The events that day haven't lost a drop of colour. They're vivid the way the world looks when you suddenly surface after swimming underwater. I must have been paying a certain kind of attention. Why, I don't know. Unless you believe that stuff. I've been over these details a million times. Because if I had done anything differently, if I had taken *this* street instead of *that* street, if I'd lingered over the lines in the fruit stall a few moments longer, then what happened would not have happened. It's like watching *Romeo and Juliet*: even though you know the story backwards, you keep hoping that *this* time the Friar will get the letter to Romeo.

"I took a morning sketch class at the Institute. We were drawing a bare-breasted

Mexican girl with a beauty spot on her right
shoulder. She had a gap between her front teeth
and you could see by the way she smiled that
she was shy about it. After the class, some of the
students, mostly women, stayed on to talk to the
instructor, a Frenchman who smoked Gauloises
through an absurdly long cigarette filter. But
I had things to do. I bought fruit for the party
in the *mercado* and then I met Jan Trober for a
coffee at the Cucaracha. She was a New York
actress who had settled in San Miguel after the
bottom fell out of her career and her husband
left her. We sat at a table on the sidewalk so we
could see all the people in the town square. The
boys walking in a circle one way, girls walking in
a circle the other; everybody eyeing each other.
Beautiful in its way, the way life works like that."

The candle sputtered and went out. We sat
in the silence and the darkness. After a while, I
said, "Shall I light another candle?"

"No, let's just sit here like this for a while."

In the hallway, voices speaking an Indian
dialect passed by the door. It's going to be
dark in here tomorrow night, I thought. And
for a few nights afterwards; and everything
will be different. You assume things are going
to be a certain way afterwards, and then you
find out, like Macbeth did, that they're not.
Preposterously not. The act, or its after-burn
rather, *becomes* who you are.

How could I have been so naive?

"In Mexico, up in the mountains where I
lived, I sometimes felt as if I had just emigrated
from a country where it always rained," Sally
said. And it seemed as though I had overheard
her thinking, that she hadn't actually meant to
say anything.

A door shut with a bang and the Indian
voices disappeared.

And Sally, where will she be? I mean physi-
cally. And that too seemed like an extraordinary
thing *not* to have considered. Because you don't

just go into the air when you die; you go other places first, and they're not so pleasant.

In the darkness, she continued. "Freddie lived on a narrow, windy cobblestone street a few blocks up from the cathedral. He found it comforting, he said, all that redemption so close at hand. He invited all his friends to the party. By sunset, his patio looked like Fire Island. Those tans, those biceps, those white teeth. There were other people too. A Brit with a pirate's moustache, a sixties rock star from some California band, a handful of alcoholic writers who had spent the morning in the Cucaracha talking about their unfinished Ph.D.s. There was a mysterious, tall Canadian who wouldn't let anyone take his picture. Some people said he was CIA. I think he'd just been thwarted by life in Toronto and was trying to make himself seem interesting. There was a retired Australian ambassador—some sort of scandal there, I forget what.

"Oh yes, and divorcees! God, so many divorcees. Women with short haircuts and children in Ivy League schools. For them, San Miguel was the last stop before the Pacific Ocean. Their last chance for a slow dance. Even if it meant sleeping with the gardener at night and letting him watch television by the pool all day long. These were *transactions*, yes, but that doesn't mean they weren't friendly, even loving. And let's face it, a friendly body in the bed is a friendly body in the bed; after a certain age, who cares why it's there.

"I was cutting limes in the kitchen with Freddie when I recognized a voice in the other room. It was a friend from Toronto who was passing through San Miguel, had stopped for a drink at the Cucaracha and somebody told her about Freddie's party.

"I heard her say, 'I hope you don't mind me crashing in like this.' I came out of the kitchen, and I was just moving through the living room when I tripped on the carpet, hit my head on the fireplace and broke my neck.

"I didn't know it was broken at the time. But I knew something bad had happened because I heard a sound I had never heard before. I've talked to other people who broke their necks and they say the same thing: in that sound, you know your life is never going to be the same again.

"I lay there for I don't know how long. There were heads appearing and disappearing above me, but the whole time my body was capable of only one sensation, and that sensation was not pain, it was dread, a sensation that said, like a blunt instrument banging under the floor, *This is a very bad thing, this is a very bad thing, this is a very bad thing.*

"I heard the voices in the room go silent, like lifting a needle off a record, and that frightened me. And it seemed that I heard Bruce breathing through his nose and saying to someone, *She brought this on herself.*

"And then I heard other voices, the kind you hear on television. 'Don't move her, don't move her.' It occurred to me, even there on the floor, that it sounded like television because it *was* from television. Like 'Boil some water.' People are always telling people to boil water on television."

She breathed deeply and after a pause said, "We should light another candle now. There's a box of them near the Drambuie. Over the fridge. They're made from beeswax."

I pulled down a red candle, unwrapped it from the delicate tissue paper it was covered with and put it on the table between us.

"There's no paraffin in beeswax candles," Sally said. "They're better for the health. More ions. Or fewer. Whichever."

I lit the candle with a long kitchen match. We watched the wick gradually change shape as the flame caught and gathered brightness. I was suddenly exhausted.

"It's incredible, isn't it?" she said.

"What?"

"How people could be so cruel that they could burn another human being alive."

"Good heavens."

"You know who I'm thinking of. *Whom*, rather."

"Yes."

"Poor little thing. What was she—fourteen?"

"Something like that."

"Will you stay the night here? All this booze, I'm going to have to take a pee."

"Of course."

"Don't leave before me." She smiled at her own joke.

I opened my lips to respond but didn't.

"When people ask me about the accident—?" she said, her voice rising into a question at the end of the phrase.

"Yes."

"How I broke my neck at a cocktail party?"

"Yes."

"They never *say* it, but I know that they assume I was drunk."

"Really?"

"I think they rather *hope* I was."

"Why would they hope that?"

"Because it's less tragic," she said.

"How would it be less tragic?"

"If I was drunk, they could think, Well, she was partly responsible."

"But if you were sober . . ."

"If I was sober, then it makes the whole thing, and the consequences that flowed out of it, arbitrary."

"The consequences?"

"Paralysis. A ruined life. That's how *they* see it, not me."

"Did you ever?" I said.

"See it as a ruined life? Oh heavens, yes. But that changed. But even after all these years, when I first meet people—?"

"Yes?"

"I feel compelled to explain that I wasn't drunk. That I was just about to have my first margarita. That's what I was doing in the kitchen with Freddie—making margaritas."

"Why do you feel compelled to tell them that?"

"Because I don't want them to think poorly of me."

"I doubt if they'd do that." My eyes settled on the cloth figure of the mischievous whale. Red seagulls soared overhead. What was he winking about? What is the secret that he and I supposedly share? "Everybody's gotten drunk at one point or another," I said.

I could feel a story insinuating itself onto my tongue, how, years before, I had gone to the washroom on the dark second-floor hallway of a Queen Street bar. Someone had forgotten to rope off the back stairs, and on my way to the washroom, a little unsteady on my feet, I turned right instead of left and tumbled face first down

the stairs to the bottom landing. I scrambled
to my feet, as if by getting up quickly I might
prevent some physical damage, the possibility of
which had already passed.

I was uninjured, not even a bruise. But the
event has stayed with me over the years, and
I still revisit it at peculiar times: during a bout
of insomnia or an afternoon daydream while
the snow is falling. I suspect it was my being so
drunk that saved me—I should have broken my
neck, but I bounced like rubber. Bump, bump,
bump, thud! It occurs to me, in those four a.m.
bouts where your thoughts seem always to land
on the wrong foot no matter where they start,
that I am as haunted these days by the catastro-
phes that *didn't* happen or *almost* happened as
I am by the ones that did. Is it, I wonder, that
dark hour alone which sends you so far afield in
pursuit of such things, such ugly little flowers?
Why does one never think of these things in
the daylight?

I kept the story to myself for the simple reason that I was in the company of a woman who had been the victim of a less colourful incident (carpet, fireplace) but the manifestations of which had disfigured her life in a matter of seconds. What does such an event say? Is the lure of religion some kind of protection from such a thing happening? From the despair that it *could* happen? *Does* happen? Why would I walk away from my accident and she didn't walk away from hers? So there can't be an afterlife, I thought. Because that would mean there has to be a God. And what kind of God would allow such a thing to happen? In what way is such an incident instructive?

"You've gone off somewhere," Sally said. "Where did you go?"

"I'm not sure."

"Yes, you are."

I grabbed the handle, so to speak, of the first pot I could reach, the recent death of a casual acquaintance, Bobby Coatsworth. Brain cancer.

He was a television news anchorman with such a deep broadcaster's voice that sometimes you couldn't quite believe he wasn't putting you on. The cancer started in his throat and bounced around his body like a pinball. Killed him in ten months. When I heard the news, I said, Well, Bobby was always a pretty tense guy. As if his being tense was why he got cancer. And why *I* didn't.

As I talked, Sally leaned forward in her chair, testing her elbow on an embroidered pillow. She was looking at me closely, waiting for something. I went on, "You hear about a plane crash, you want to know immediately where the plane was coming from, or where it was going to."

"Really?"

"Because—because then you think, I never go *there* anyway."

"Did you think that when the Air France plane went down last summer?"

"I did. I thought, Well shit, they were going

to São Paulo. As if going to São Paulo had anything to do with the cargo door falling off over
the Atlantic."

"Did you feel that way about my accident?
That I had it coming?"

"Never. Not for a second."

"I wonder why not."

"Because I love you."

It didn't make any sense, it didn't follow
anything, but I've always been glad I said it,
always been glad it just blurted out.

The telephone rang. The purring kind. *Purr.*
Pause. *Purr, purr.*

"Let it go," she said. "I'm having too much
fun."

Like waiting for a waiter to finish pouring
the wine and leave the table, we waited for the
phone to stop.

"Did you have anything in your hands?"
I said.

"What?"

"When you tripped on the carpet in Mexico, did you have anything in your hands?"

"That's a question no one's ever asked me."

"Perhaps it's not so interesting a question."

"Why do you ask?"

"I have often wondered why you didn't throw your hands up to protect your face. Or was it all too fast?"

"No, it wasn't too fast," she said in the tones of one who is deciding whether or not to pursue a subject. "You know why I didn't throw my hands up? I didn't throw my hands up because I was born with an eccentric deficiency. Move a little closer to me."

I hesitated. "Is this going to be something that hurts?"

"I don't do things like that. I hate people who do things like that. But come a little closer."

I got up and stood above her.

"Bend down a bit."

"Sally."

"Trust me."

I bent over. She took one of my hands and moved it toward her face. She did it the first time slowly, the second time a little faster. "When I was born, I was born without a reflex to protect my face. I wore glasses in high school and when I was playing sports. I didn't need them, but if something lurched at my face, I didn't react."

Then she took my hand—her hand was very warm, the fingers curled inward but her fingernails were beautifully maintained—and moved it slowly toward my face. I think it was more of a reason to touch me, to have me touch her, than to illustrate what she meant. But I was glad to do it. Glad to touch her. I thought to myself, Am I the last person who will ever touch you? Is mine the final human contact? I let her hand rest on my face.

She said, "Whereas if I make a motion toward your face, you'll put up your hands, you'll blink."

I pulled my eyes away from her. I could feel my chest tighten. I said, "You never told me that before." I sat back down.

"Where was I?" she asked.

"You were lying on the dining room floor of Freddie's house."

"A local doctor arrived. He gave me a shot. I woke up in a helicopter. It took me from San Miguel to the ABC hospital in Mexico City."

"Didn't you have to pee by then?"

"Everything had shut down. From my neck downwards. It was like waking up in somebody else's sleeping body. You want to move your arm, but your arm won't obey, as if it has forgotten the language the two of you spoke and all it hears now is gibberish.

"Three or four doctors came in. They spoke only in English, even when they were talking to each other. A very classy gesture—they didn't want me wondering what was being said. Still, I did have the feeling that I had become somehow the object of a Martian science experiment. A doctor brushed the sole of my foot with what looked like a Popsicle stick. 'Does that tickle?' he said. And I kept saying, 'Have you done it yet, have you done it yet?' And then they switched to my other foot, same business, and there was something about the matter-of-factness, the *professional* matter-of-factness with which they responded to my question *Have you done it yet?* that filled me with a kind of dull fright, as if the fright itself was a piece of lead in my body.

"I asked them a question. *The* question. But they wouldn't answer it. They put me in a long metal tube with lights inside and a round window. Like a small spaceship. Sometimes I was looking at the ceiling tiles, other times I was looking at the floor tiles. Like a human sausage on a rotisserie.

"The next day or the day after, a doctor came in to see me. He was a lanky man with thick grey hair, like a movie star playing a

Mexican doctor. Dr. Philippe Ortoya. He flirted with me. Maybe it was therapy. While he was checking my pupils, I said, 'I want you to tell me the truth, Doctor. Will I ever run down the street again?'

"'No,' he said.

"'Will I ever climb the stairs to my bedroom on the second floor?'

"'I'm afraid not,' he said.

"'Will I ever be able to go to the bathroom without a bag on my leg?'

"He said, 'It's too early to tell.'

"I said, 'Is that the best news you have for me?'

"Dr. Ortoya seemed to understand what I was thinking, because he said to me, 'We get used to situations.'

"'Not this situation.'

"He said, 'Do nothing rash. Wait.'

"I said to him, 'Is there anything to wait for?'

"'Are you religious?'

"When I heard that, I thought, Boy oh boy, am I ever going to kill myself! Suddenly, there was a real urgency to do it—to do it quickly, before anybody could read my mind and stop me. But that's the problem with being crippled: You can't kill yourself. The best you can do is fall out of your bed and bang your head on the floor. But that's not going to kill you.

"And you can't ask a friend to roll you to the edge of a cliff and look away for a second. Because even then, you can't get out of your fucking chair. You have to have someone *tip* you. And, you know, finding someone to tip you over the side of a cliff, that's a tall order. Those kinds of friends are hard to come by.

"One night, as I lay in my hospital bed in Mexico City, I watched a romance start up in the building across the street between a man with a mop and a bucket—he must have been new on the job—and a woman in a blue apron who was going from office to office emptying the

wastepaper baskets. It was the middle of the
night, just their floor was illuminated, and you
could see them working their way toward each
other. The one thing that nothing, not even
gravity, can stop: people finding their way to
each other even in a dark building. It went for
a week like this, the two of them meeting in
the brightly lit office and talking. And then one
night I saw the man get up and go over and turn
off the lights. Just for a half-hour or so. And I
wondered if, in my condition, I would ever be
part of that world again. Would I—" Here she
paused, as if the instant in which the original
thought had first occurred to her reopened like a
seed in her memory. "Would I ever be attractive
to the opposite sex again?

"Sometimes, when I opened my eyes, I
expected to discover myself back in Toronto. As
if Mexico and Freddie Steigman and my patio
looking at the mountains and the party and the
limes on the cutting board and the knock at the

door and the carpet and the voices going silent
were the kind of unhealthy fog you drift around
in when you have slept too long. A progression
into staleness.

"But then I'd glance around my room, I'd
hear Spanish voices in the hallway, and I'd
think, This can't possibly have happened to
me. You go to a party, you cross the room, you
trip on the carpet. Do you know how many
coincidences have to happen for you to arrive
there? But there is no reward in figuring out the
statistics, is there? Because it all returns you to
here and now.

"I woke up once after midnight. My legs
were on fire. Some terrible, insistent pain, like
an animal staring at me from the doorway. I lay
there listening to the soft swish of white shoes
outside my room, back and forth, back and forth.
I thought, I'm going to lie here very still and this
thing will go away; it'll get bored and go away.
But it didn't. It just sort of flopped itself across

the doorway with a grunt and waited. Pain, I'm telling you—pain and the things that come with pain—it's such a horribly *private* business. I'm sure for some people that the actual act of dying is a relief. If only to extinguish those monotonous, incommunicable, repetitive cartoons.

"I pushed a button on a cord and an angel appeared at the side of my bed. She gave me a fat pink pill. It left a bitter taste at the back of my throat, even with a glass of water, but I suspected that good things would come with that taste. And they did. I couldn't tell if I was asleep or awake, but I could actually *watch* my thoughts take on a physical shape, even colour, like people in a novel who suddenly forget they're characters and start moving around on their own. Pursuing their own concerns.

"I buzzed the nurse. I asked her to raise up my bed as high as it would go, to prop me up on pillows so that the whole of Mexico City lay below me. It must have been a Saturday night.

The town was lit up like a pulsing Christmas
tree, and I felt like something very good was just
about to happen to me. Somebody was playing
the piano. How perfect, and yet how odd—a
piano on a hospital ward in the middle of the
night.

"I thought about Dr. Ortoya in his crisp
linen jacket, about the angel in the whisper-
ing shoes, about all the life in Mexico City. In
the bars, in the streets, in the cantinas, in the
houses—all this glittering, energized life. I
thought of Chloe, smiling in her sleep. And I
thought, This is a good deal, being alive. Life is
a good deal.

"But the next day, things didn't seem so
cheerful. And even in that clear sunlight, the
banality of the world seemed like the dominant
chord." Here, Sally paused for a moment. "Or
perhaps *because* of the sunlight," she added privately. "Do you understand me?"

"Yes."

"Perhaps it was my third day in the hospital. A grey day outside my window. The city flat, lifeless. All night long, a man across the hall with a bullet wound in his thigh had been groaning. I didn't hear him come in. I was dreaming about lying on a dock at the edge of a country lake. You were there. So was your older brother, Jake. We were all tanned. Tanned and skinny. I could hear the wind passing through the pine trees on the shore. You know that sound it makes, that swish, the pine needles rubbing their hands together.

"I was lying face down; I could smell the sun-bleached wood; I could hear the water lapping under the dock. Little by little, the groaning of the man in the hospital bed across the hall began to mingle with the sounds I could hear on the dock: a boat crossing the bay, the water lapping under the boards, the wind in the pine trees, a man groaning with a bullet in his thigh.

"I woke up. Rain splattered on the hospital windows—fat, dull-witted drops. *Splat, splat, splat,* not like regular rain, but like transparent jelly thrown at the glass. *Splat, splat, splat.* The pill had worn off, leaving behind a sort of flatness like a winter field that stretches all the way to the horizon. And I thought that this is what life is like without my pill, this field that you walk across forever. Yes, I'm going to use all my intelligence, all my creativity, to put an end to this. I was, at that very second, wondering how to get more pills out of my angel when a girl as thin as a pencil appeared in the doorway. It was my daughter, Chloe.

"'How are you feeling, Mama?' she said, and the sound of her voice, with its tiny, uncertain wobble, broke my heart. It just cut me in half, and within seconds I realized that all my plans, my schemes, my scenarios for killing myself, were suddenly in the back seat, suddenly in the past tense. Inconceivable. Like a drunken fantasy from whose grips you awake thinking, What in Heaven's name was all *that* about?

"If grown-ups can get used to new and dreadful circumstances fast, children do it with a speed that's breathtaking. They really *are* built for survival. It was like watching an eyeball come into focus, the way Chloe accepted the new version of me—the neck brace, crabbed hands, the motionless legs.

"There she was, perched like a bird on the side of my bed, talking about a red-haired girl at the American school she attended in San Miguel, about why so many boys liked her. What is it about some girls that boys like? she wondered. And I could see that she was completely absorbed by the red-haired girl. The sun came back out and transformed the city into a dazzling foreign port."

Three

Eighteen floors down from Sally's apartment, a car alarm went off in the parking lot. *Honk, honk, honk, honk.* We both listened to it involuntarily. Then it suddenly stopped and the room again filled with silence, a more profound silence, it seemed, both of us privately aware of where we were and why we were there. In only a few hours, we had grown so enthralled with each other's company that the third person in the room had disappeared.

"I wrote the note," she said.

"What's it say?"

"Just to call the police before coming into the apartment."

"Okay."

"I don't want to make any troubles for you," she said.

"Okay."

"Just stick it to the door when you leave."

"Are you sure you want to do this, Sally?"

"It's not complicated," she said evenly, and I had the feeling she had said this before, but only to herself, in preparation for this very conversation. "I'm not depressed, the world isn't grey, I don't want to punish people, it's just that this"—she gestured toward her body in the green dressing gown—"has become less and less manageable. I don't want to go into physical details, but you understand. And it's only going to get worse. And soon—not tomorrow or even next year, soon though—I won't have even this much control over what happens to me. And then there's you," she added softly.

"What about me?"

"One of these days, you might go away. Or you might change your mind."

"And?"

"And then I wouldn't have anyone to help me."

"Is there no one else?"

"I can't imagine there would be. Could you?"

"How did you know I wouldn't tell someone?" I said.

She was looking right at me now. She waited a moment. "Because I know what you're like. Because enough is enough."

The phone rang.

"Do you want to get that?"

But she didn't answer. She had retreated into herself, and I suddenly had the feeling she was thinking about her son, Kyle. But I didn't want to bring him up. Not tonight. She seemed to read my thoughts, though, and taking a deep, involuntary breath as one does before beginning a task that has been done before but needs to be done again, she began. "About six months after my accident, I got a letter from my ex-husband, Bruce. Chloe

and I had moved back to the house in San Miguel.
I was in a wheelchair, but managing."

The phone stopped ringing.

"It was a disturbing but not a surprising
letter, something I had expected for some time.
Kyle, who was seventeen, had gotten himself
into trouble. Teenage trouble. But from the
lugubrious and self-satisfied tones of his father's
letter, you'd have thought it was murder. None
of which would have happened, it implied, if I
hadn't *whored* off to Mexico."

"Did he use that expression?"

"No." Pause. "That's mine."

"Go on."

"Kyle and a couple of his goony friends
from the neighbourhood got drunk one night at
some girl's house—her parents were away—and
broke into their own school. Their *own* school.
They wandered around the halls, trashed a few
lockers, pissed in the water fountain, smashed a
mirror in the girls' washroom and then drifted

downstairs into the basement. There, at the far end of the school, they found themselves in the music room. The door was unlocked. Inside, they came across five electric guitars that had been rented for an upcoming student performance. Somebody said, 'Are you thinking what I'm thinking?' So they stole the guitars, slipping out the tradesmen's entrance.

"Bruce was out of town, working with a highway crew up near Lake Athabasca, so they took their loot back to his house. Kyle was a lot of things, but he wasn't stupid, and when he woke up hungover the next morning, he realized that he was in real trouble, that he had to do something to fix it.

"His friends had stayed overnight, but they were morons—Kyle's friends generally were—and when he asked them for help, they sat with their fingers up their asses and then buggered off. So there was Kyle, with five stolen guitars heating up his bedroom like a hothouse.

"What do you do? He came up with an idea. He found the vice-principal's number in the phone book and called him at home. He claimed that a buddy of his—he couldn't name him— had gotten drunk, broken into the school and stolen some stuff. Now, in a fit of remorse, he wanted to return them, with Kyle as the inter- mediary. Could this be arranged discreetly?

"The VP said sure. But when Kyle arrived in a taxi half an hour later, the five guitars stacked like corpses in the back seat, he found two plain- clothes detectives waiting for him on the front steps of the school. They took him downstairs into the music room and grilled him. No win- dows, just the two cops, the vice-principal, and Kyle reeking of gin. A cop with a shiny, fleshy face started things off. It was pretty obvious, he said, that Kyle was a prankster who'd gone on a toot. He could smell it from here. But there was no way that his so-called 'buddy' had got these guitars out the door, up an embankment, across a playing field all on his own. Not unless he was 'a fucking octopus.'

"So he must have had some help. *Kyle's* help. So why didn't Kyle just come clean and help everyone 'straighten this out' so they could close the book on it. No harm done. Just kids being kids.

"But Kyle, having already been lied to once that day by the vice-principal, wasn't buying. He stuck to his story. He didn't know what happened, didn't know how they got the guitars out of the school, he was just there doing a favour.

"Consulting a notebook, the fleshy cop said, 'It says here a Hammond organ was stolen as well.'

"'There was no organ,' Kyle said.

"'Are you sure?'

"Kyle didn't see the trap. 'Yes, I'm sure.'

"'Well,' the cop said, 'if you weren't there, how would you know that an organ wasn't stolen too?'

"His partner stepped in. 'Listen, fuckweed, if I don't have the name of the thief on this piece of paper in thirty seconds, I will charge *you* with grand theft, possession of stolen property, intent to traffic, and you will, I promise, go to jail.' He gave him a good poke in the chest with his finger just to show he meant business.

"'Arrest me, then,' Kyle said. 'Arrest me and fuck you.'"

"He said that?"

"That's what he said he said."

"Ballsy little guy."

"The police must have thought so too, because they let him go. For the moment. The fleshy cop said, 'I'm going to give you twenty-four hours, Kyle. Then I'm going to come to your house, and I'm going to arrest you in front of your parents and your neighbours. I'm going to put you in handcuffs, and I'm going to take you to jail.'

"His partner said, 'You ever hear of grand theft, you little fuck? That's theft over a thousand dollars. You're in the big leagues now. You can thank your buddies for letting you take it in the ass for them. Because that's where you're headed. You know how long a kid like you will last in jail?'"

I'd forgotten what a skilful mimic Sally could be. She didn't do it very often; it wasn't her style, too attention-getting a number for her. But as a child, those times I saw her do it, saw her cut loose some night and "do" a neighbour talking to herself while gardening or our soused uncle saying good night but not leaving, I'd find myself staring at her as if I were watching a chair levitate.

She went on. "Kyle went home. He didn't tell his father, nor did he sleep that night, not a wink, just a tumble of awful imaginings. Exactly twenty-four hours later, he sat by the front door with his night kit packed—pyjamas,

hairbrush, toothpaste, toothbrush—and waited
to be taken to what he imagined was some kind
of Russian gulag.

"The appointed hour arrived. Five o'clock.
Then five-fifteen. Then six o'clock. Kyle walked
down to the sidewalk and peered up and down
the street. Nothing. No one. They never came.

"But after, he refused to go back to school.
To *any* school. That's what Bruce's letter was
about. He suggested that Kyle come down to
Mexico and live with me. Asked me to take
some time to think about it. I didn't need
time. But I pretended to, pretended that I had
reservations: the wheelchair, not being up on
crutches yet and so on. In fact, what I didn't
want was for Bruce to realize how *thrilled* I was
to have *both* my children down there with me.
I thought if he even smelt it, something would
go tight in his chest and he'd snatch it away.
But I don't know. Maybe I was doing him a dis-
service. Now that he's gone, he seems like less

of an asshole and more a product of growing up in a small town.

"A few weeks later, Kyle arrived on the afternoon bus. It was spring now, the days very hot. Freddie Steigman and Chloe went down to the depot to pick him up. On the way home, Freddie read him the riot act. He said, 'You have no idea what trouble is like until you've been on the inside of a Mexican jail.'

"It must have been three or four nights later when Kyle and an American kid went into a cantina and drank a half-dozen rounds of mescal. Around midnight, they dropped in on a girl they'd met that morning. But the girl's father answered the door and, seeing that they were drunk, sent them packing. Here the story gets fuzzy. Kyle always claimed his friend did it, his friend said Kyle did it, but somebody threw a brick through the girl's window. The police were called. They picked up the two boys in a cantina down the street. At four o'clock in the morning,

there was a knock on my door. There was Kyle.
They'd roughed him up a bit. He had a black eye
and a loose front tooth. Luckily, he had mentioned Freddie Steigman's name.

"The next day, I made my decision, and I've
been living with the consequences of it since then.
I packed up his little suitcase and put him on a
bus back to the airport. I've often thought about
it—maybe I should have kept him. But I was
too vulnerable, too weak to deal with a six-foot-
tall teenager crashing around town and getting
in trouble and maybe, just maybe, getting us all
thrown out of the country. Was I a coward? Was I
using the wheelchair as an excuse to not deal with
a troubled—and more to the point, trouble*some*—
teenager? Did I abandon my son? Was I playing
the ostrich when I sent him back to his father? Am
I responsible for what happened afterwards?"

"Probably not," I said.

"It doesn't change anything anyway. Things
went the way they went."

"And how was that?"

"You know the answer to that," she said flatly.

"Yes, but how did they get there?"

"Kyle got a job in Toronto looking after senior citizens in a Jewish retirement home. He'd take them out for walks, wheel them around the block in their wheelchairs, talk to them on the bench in front of the home and read their granddaughters' letters aloud to them.

"He was a prince, everyone loved him— until they discovered he was stealing their medication. Librium, Valium, Seconal, Mandrax, Dilaudid, even cough medicine—anything he could find. They were seniors. Have you ever seen the medicine cabinet of a senior?"

"Yes, I have, in fact."

"Then you know. The pickings are good.

"The police were called in. They installed a hidden camera in the bathroom of one of the most frequently hit rooms, and waited. Sure enough, while Mrs. Cornblum was downstairs enjoying Shabbat dinner with her son and her grandchildren, Kyle was systematically going through the prescription bottles in her medicine cabinet. All on film. The police turned up at his house with a search warrant. They found jewellery, a necklace, even a silver pocket watch, very old and valuable, which had been stolen that same morning. A few pills, but not many. Kyle had taken them or sold them.

"The judge was a softie and handed down a conditional discharge. Kyle walked out of the courthouse with a slap on the wrist. Bruce threw him out. He flopped here and there, always with these losers. Kyle had a knack for attracting dumb-guy groupies. A string of arrests followed: shoplifting, breaking into cars, selling phony prescription pads, phone scams. One time he even got caught for stealing purses from cars in a cemetery parking lot while their occupants were paying graveside respects."

"A perfect little scumball."

Sally frowned; it hurt her to hear that. You can say bad things about your own child, but you don't want someone else doing it.

"Sally, I apologize. I was just getting into the spirit of things."

She went on. "He landed in the hospital a few times. A furniture mover caught him breaking into his rig, this big-bellied, thick-armed ape who made his living driving to Mississippi and back on three hundred ciga-rettes and a handful of Dexedrine. Wrong guy to rob. Wrong guy to get *caught* robbing. He found Kyle sitting behind the wheel trying to snap off his ham radio. Kyle got so frightened he threw himself over a ramp. But it was a drop of two storeys. He broke his arm in four places. The truck driver took his time getting down to him, then gave him a couple of boots, one in the kidneys, one in the face, and left him lying in the street."

"Nice life."

"That February, he had a Methedrine overdose, his heart stopped beating on the operating table. All this got back to me in Mexico. I was torn: stay or go home. But go home and do what? Hobbling around on crutches. Shouting from the sidelines. At some point, you're reduced to being an impotent cheerleader for your children's lives. Or is that just more bullshit? I don't know. I still don't.

"I began to prepare myself for his death. I began to imagine how the phone would ring one night, or maybe Bruce's hangdog face would appear at my door in Mexico. I knew it was coming. It was the Jerry Malloy business that brought me home."

"You haven't mentioned him."

"Jerry Malloy? That was the clincher." She leaned her elbow on the chair arm; it slipped off; she settled it back again, using her other hand to hold it. She began. "One night around midnight,

Kyle turned up at Marek Grunbaum's house.
Remember him? The Polish guy—"

"—with the beautiful pink handkerchief."

"Kyle looked like a zombie: ragged clothes,
grey skin, yellow eyeballs. He smelt, too. His
feet were rotting from some untreated infec-
tion. Marek made him take his clothes off in the
hallway, all of them, and then led him naked
upstairs to the shower, disinfecting his footsteps
with an aerosol can of Lysol as he went. His
three kids peeking from their bedrooms. 'Who's
that, Daddy?' A few days later, he drove him
to a rehab centre downtown. On the way there,
Kyle asked if he could borrow twenty dollars.
A birthday present for his father. He had a con
man's charm, Kyle did. He looked Marek in the
eyes and said, 'You got to let me make this up to
my dad.'

"He disappeared into the mid-afternoon traffic with the twenty dollars. Nearly half an hour
later, after Marek had circled the block twice and

gotten a ticket, he spotted Kyle on the sidewalk.
He got back into the car, claiming he couldn't
find anything nice. But could he keep the
money? Within a day or two, he'd be allowed
out for half-hour walks in the neighbourhood—
he'd buy a present then.

"By now, Marek just wanted him out of the
car. So he agreed. He pulled up in front of the
clinic, a big white house on a leafy street. He
waited to make sure Kyle went in. Kyle skipped
up the main stairs, made a theatrical production
of pushing the buzzer, and, just as he went in,
spun around and gave Marek a grin and a big
wave, as if this was all a screech, just too much
fun for words.

"They lodged Kyle with a boy named Jerry
Malloy. Jerry had grown up in one of those small
northern towns where teenage boys sit in front of
the pizza parlour at midnight on a Saturday night,
daydreaming about the life they've read about in
heavy metal magazines. You know those kids?"

"I sure do."

"You see them in all small towns. You can smell the boredom coming off them. They usually get arrested for breaking into somebody's cottage, knock up the girl at the grocery store, put on forty pounds, spend their lives working at the marina or the planing mill. I have a great deal of compassion for those children." Sally looked toward the window, and in a moment continued. "But not Jerry. Jerry saw himself as a cut above the rest. No marina for him. He quit school in grade ten and moved to Toronto, where he got a job making broom handles in a factory.

"It wasn't long before big-city life just dazzled the wits right out of him. Especially the drugs, of course, first pot, then Methedrine—"

"Nasty business, that Methedrine."

"—then whatever he could get his big farm-boy fingers around. It was all good, all part of an adventure that put another square on the checkerboard between him and the boys in front of the pizza parlour back home.

"Whacked on sleeping pills one day, he stole a car that had been double-parked with the engine running. He drove it the wrong way down a one-way street, spotted a police van (which was empty, by the way), panicked and smacked into a fire hydrant. Totalled the car. Knocked himself out cold. Chipped his front teeth on the driver's wheel.

"The judge, realizing he was dealing with a moron, gave Jerry a choice: jail or rehab. To his misfortune, Jerry Malloy, the boy who made broomsticks, chose rehab. And to punish him for his crimes, they put him in with my son.

"Kyle was everything that Jerry imagined a city boy would be: slick and quick with a put-down, always on the hustle. He was smitten. For his part, Kyle knew he had fallen on a live one and treated Jerry like a goofy sheepdog. Had him doing his chores, cleaning the toilet, making

the beds—the things you do in rehab to reac-
quaint yourself with regular life. Kyle wasn't
interested in regular life.

"Three or four weeks in, I got a call from
Bruce. It turned out that Kyle had smuggled
two grams of Lebanese hash into the centre.
He'd bought them on the street with Marek's
twenty dollars. Smuggled them past security in
the loose portion of his shoe sole, grinning and
joking with the guard. It must have been the
excitement of it all, making a fool of everybody, that explained Kyle's wild wave to Marek
as he went in.

"And then one night, after everyone had
gone to sleep on his floor, he stole out of bed,
recovered the hashish and offered a drag to
Jerry. Within three hours, they were caught
breaking into the meat fridge in the basement,
but not before Kyle had turned on a young
amphetamine addict from Stratford and a sixty-
eight-year-old alcoholic. Within the space of a

few hours, Kyle had undone months and months
of rehabilitation.

"It was an act of such egregious irresponsi-
bility that the centre gave up on him. You can fix
an addict, but you can't fix an asshole. Both of
them got kicked out, Kyle and Jerry. Then, poof,
they vanished. For a couple of weeks, no one
heard from them. Maybe they went to Jerry's
hometown. I don't know. No one heard from
Kyle—not his father, not his friends, not me,
no one. So how what happened next happened
isn't entirely clear. But you can guess the broad
strokes: Kyle had found a mark and wrung him
like a washcloth for everything he could get.

"Before too long, probably at Kyle's suggestion, Jerry stole his uncle's pickup truck. He
must have figured he was in a movie, two ban-
dits on the run. They turned up at a local dog
pound, adopted a mongrel and began to wind
their way across Canada. They were heading
to Vancouver. Somebody had told them it was

like Florida there, warm temperatures, pretty
girls—they'd get a job on a fishing boat and sail
to China. Butch Cassidy and the Sundance Kid.

"They went up around the Great Lakes into
Manitoba. Stealing gas when they needed it.
Shoplifting here and there, mostly smash-and-
grab. A farm family reported that a couple of
young guys, one with chipped front teeth, stayed
with them for several days, stole their grandson's
coin collection and moved on. The people who
were kind to Kyle were people, he figured, who
had targets on their backs, suckers who were
saying, 'Here, fuck me, I'm stupid.'

"Jerry turned a trick in a truck stop outside
Winnipeg, let some guy blow him in the back of
his rig, and that got them another seventy-five
dollars. They made it as far as the outskirts of a
town just across the Alberta border. They were
driving at night. Kyle was. He fell asleep, the
truck left the road, rolled down an embankment,
turned over three or four times, killed Jerry and

killed the dog. The police picked up Kyle half a
mile away, hitchhiking."

Here Sally cocked her head as if she were
trying to recall something, a gesture I remembered from my childhood. "Chloe and I gave
up the house in San Miguel a little while after.
The town was haunted for me, like a before-
and-after photograph. And when Freddie died
(his cleaning lady found him on his bed in a
blue linen jacket: he must have lain down for a
moment to catch his breath and never gotten up
again, dear Freddie), there was nothing to keep
me there.

"I rented an apartment at the edge of Forest
Hill Village. The poor part. Still, it was com-
forting to be neighbours to so many Mercedes
and pretty gardens. It was an old-style brick
building in slight disrepair, with lead windows.
Remember those? Kyle was back in Toronto too.
He wanted to move in with us. At first, I said no.
Absolutely not.

"There were tears, of course, then accusa-
tions. I'd deserted him in Mexico, left him with
a harsh father. Had loved Chloe more than him.
While he was talking, I had, for the first time
ever, a sensation in my body that I was dealing
with a pathological liar. A liar whose charm and
intelligence had become a sort of lubricant for
getting whatever he was trying to get. Do you
understand what I'm saying? I'm saying for the
first time it occurred to me that for my beloved
son Kyle, language, the words that you actually *use*, was simply a kind of camouflage that
allowed him to be a predator without seeming to
be a predator. Even his tears seemed self-serving.
As though he was lying, knew he was lying, but
didn't care. Was only concerned with the success
of the performance."

"But you loved him."

"Yes. Everything just flew out the window
in his presence, and I'd think, He's so fabulous.
I kept thinking, This is circumstantial. But then

I'd overhear him on the phone and I'd think, Who is this? Is this a mask? Where is the little boy who was scared of ghost stories, and who was so shy at summer camp that he was scared to ask where the toilets were?"

"Did it occur to you that he was crazy or an addict?"

"It occurred to me he was a little pig with his nose in the trough. A shameless, self-gratifying bag of appetites. And that once he understood this—that that was how the world was coming to see him—his vanity would stop him."

"Makes sense."

"Only on paper. *Only on paper.* I took him out to dinner. Taxis, crutches, the whole business. I wanted to be somewhere fresh with him, somewhere that didn't smell like my apartment. I asked him when was the last time he was happy. He lied at first, gave me some fiction he thought I wanted to hear. I stopped him. I said, 'Stop lying to me. It's killing me. It's killing *us.*'

"So he said with this goofy grin, 'Breaking into a car, I suppose. Well, not exactly breaking in, but that moment when you look in the window, see something you like, look up and down the street, the coast is clear, and then you *do* it.'

"I asked if he was saying that to shock me. It wasn't the criminality of it that was so distressing, it was the vulgarity, the sheer vulgarity of it, and the strange gleam of pleasure that he got in his eyes when he said it. He looked . . . *feral.* I said, 'Was *that* really the last time you were happy?'

"He thought for a moment and he said, 'Yeah, it really was, Mom.'

"'Don't you want to change your life?' I said. 'No, not really.' I asked him if he thought he was going to live to be an old man. He said he didn't think about it much. I said, 'What *do* you think about, Kyle, when you wake up at four o'clock in the morning and you're in some dirty little rooming house with needles on the table and bloodstains on the wall?'

"He seemed perplexed by the question, and I realized that something had shut down in him. That his fine intelligence had dimmed, and, I suspected, dimmed irretrievably. It was hard to admit it, but I wasn't sitting in a restaurant with a skeletal young man whose wit used to make even the police do a double take. I was having dinner instead with a common, dull-witted television watcher. A *chronic* television watcher. Getting high, watching television, breaking into cars, getting high, watching television. That was it. That was his whole life."

"You must have grown to loathe him."

"No, no, I never did. Not for long, anyway. I couldn't help feeling that there was a magic key out there, that if I could just find it and put it in the lock, the door would open and everything would change."

"And?"

"Mothers are fools for their sons. I let him move in. I couldn't leave him wandering the

streets—I was afraid he'd get killed. He had
known intuitively which nerves to pluck, especially that business about sending him home
from Mexico. He camped out on my couch,
making up his bed in the morning. For a while it
worked. Chloe went to school; I took a Spanish
course. I was hoping one day maybe I could
go back to Mexico—somewhere else, though.
Puerto Vallarta, maybe. Gay towns are always
the safest towns in foreign countries. I'd spent
most of my money, so I was living on a disabil-
ity pension."

"Why didn't you go back to making your
wall hangings?"

She looked at the winking whale, at the
red seagulls drifting over the lagoon. "I tried,
but somehow the air had just gone out of it. I
couldn't do the drawing or the cutting. I'd have
had to hire someone to do it, and that seemed
like paying someone to collect stamps for you.
But we were making out fine."

She went on. "It was a temporary arrange-
ment with Kyle, but it gave me something for
which I was hungry: it gave me *him,* his company. He had been such a bright, perceptive
little boy, so clever about his friends, his parents,
even himself. How to put it? It was so sad. He
belonged to that group, that maddening group
of people who are capable of unsparing self-
analysis but incapable of controlling the same
impulses they talk so brilliantly about. But I
loved him, and I kept waiting for him to happen on the right key for the right lock. And for a
while, it looked like he just might."

"And?"

"He joined Alcoholics Anonymous. Got a
terrific sponsor—a middle-aged businessman
who phoned him every night. He got a job in
a warehouse. Marek got it for him. He did it
for me, yes, but he believed in the magic key
too. Except his was a bit different. His was the
brutality of hard work. That Eastern European

thing. And for a long time, maybe six months, it worked.

"Kyle got himself another girlfriend. Japanese this time. Women always liked him. It was a blessing and a curse. They always wanted to save him. Including his mother. All of us believing in the magic key. One month went by; three months; six months. I could feel a belt loosening around my chest. And then, one summer morning on the way to work, he walked by a neighbourhood bar—I even remember the name, the Moonstone—and he went in.

"He must have walked by that bar, God, I don't know, a hundred times? But that day he went in. They were just setting up. He put money down on the bar and asked for a beer. The bartender asked him what he wanted. Kyle said, 'You choose something.' Unusual request. That's why later, when the guy talked to the police, he remembered Kyle."

A door opened just down the corridor from Sally's apartment. Music briefly issued onto the flowered carpet. "Come on," a young woman's voice said, "this was *your* idea, now come *on*." A dog collar rattled by the door, followed by an excited bark. "Shhh."

"Next thing we know, Kyle calls into work, says he's sick. Not a word to his sponsor, naturally. He knew the guy wouldn't buy it. Sometime around noon, Kyle ends up in a ravine with a couple of guys. The ravine right under the subway bridge that leads to GreekTown. They drink their way along the Danforth, walking out on a few bills, stop in to see one of the guy's girlfriends who works in a health spa and borrow some money from her. Somebody sells them an eight ball, crack and heroin.

"They come back across town and end up in that private school on Avenue Road. What's it called? The one you went to?"

"Upper Canada College."

"They bust into lockers looking for something to steal. They figure, because it's a private school, all these rich kids have got to be keeping bags of loose cash in their lockers. A security guy hears them, they throw a pair of soccer boots at him and hightail it out of the school. They run across a cricket pitch where there's a game on, all these guys in white flannels and cricket bats. By the time the police arrive, they've disappeared over a side fence and are hiding out in a backyard in Forest Hill. An hour later, the police get a call from a woman who says there are three naked guys swimming in her pool. They get away again.

"Two days later, a cop sees an illegally parked car with no plates on it. He opens the door. It's my baby inside. Kyle. All by himself. They figured he died somewhere else and they dumped the body in a stolen car and walked away. In his pocket—and this always breaks my

heart—is a city map, all the places he's been over
the past few days, this long arc through the city
heading back to his apartment. Inscribed on the
map were the words, *I am on a voyage of mysterious intent.* He was like a fish swimming upstream.
He thought he was going home, but he wasn't.
He was getting ready to die. And he did."

We sat in the silence for a moment; her
refrigerator came on with a hum. She said,
"I've thought about this a lot, and the truth is,
I think he knew he couldn't manage more than
six months of 'being good,' and the alternative
wasn't possible either."

Somewhere in the wall behind me, a metal
pipe clanked.

"But why do you suppose he chose *that*
morning to go into the bar? Why not the day
before? Why not the day after? You lose a child,
you keep wondering about those little things.
As though, if I could find an answer, I could
somehow make it not have happened. Which is

absurd, I know. But still, I can't seem to leave it alone."

I said nothing.

She turned her dark eyes to me. "How could his sister be his sister and he be him?"

"What do you mean?"

"They slept in the same bedroom, they had the same parents, the same amount of love, the same things for breakfast. They used the same words, they spoke with the same speech rhythms. They liked the same TV shows. They disliked the same songs on the radio. They were like a little unit moving around the house together when they were small. How could they be so similar in so many ways and yet, in that small corner of their personalities where they were unalike, be *so* unalike, and have that same unlikeness be the deciding factor in the course of their lives? Why wouldn't it be the other things, the other qualities, that set the course? Can you explain this to me?"

"I can't."

"It's the same with you and your brother, Jake. You hate each other."

I said, "I haven't talked to Jake for years. Have you?"

"Sometimes. Rarely."

"What's he like?" I asked, my voice rising half an octave, as though my body, independent of my will, was preparing to defend itself, as though the time between now and our last ugly confrontations had been reduced to a matter of days, not years.

"Unhappy. So unhappy. He's quite categorical about it. He says, 'I'm not going to be happy until I'm fifty.'"

"Why fifty?"

"I don't know. He just said it."

After a moment, I said, "What am *I* like?"

"At your best?"

"Let's start there."

"Here. You're here. And all that that— implies."

"At my worst?" I thought, Let's get it over with.

She shook her head. "You're here. That's what matters."

The elevator doors opened down the hall. Voices passed the door.

"It's late," she said. "I wonder who they are. I wonder where they're coming from."

The candle sputtered.

"Am I safe to ask you something?" she said.

"Yes."

"You're sure?"

"Yes, I'm sure."

"Will you regret this? Will you drive through this neighbourhood some night twenty years from now and regret this?"

"It doesn't matter. Not tonight."

"It's hard to imagine you in twenty years," she said. "It's hard to imagine you a day older than tonight."

"Why did you ask me if it was safe?" I said.

"Because I don't want to say the wrong thing."

"Please, Sally." I could feel my eyes watering.

"What?" she said suddenly.

"Please say whatever you want."

The phone rang again. *Purr, purr.* I raised my eyebrows at Sally. She shook her head. She knew who it was, I thought, but didn't want to tell me. Finally, it went silent. And again the room seemed preternaturally quiet.

She said, "I've got to go to the bathroom. Can you hang on?"

"Sure."

"You'll be here when I get back?"

"Yes."

Sally got up on her crutches. I put my hand under her armpit—it was warm—and steadied her. "Okay?" I said.

She stared down at the carpet. Or her slippers, I couldn't tell which. "Yep," she said, breathing in on the word the way people some-

times speak in the country, the way her grandmother spoke.

Out the window, I could see the flickering
red lights of a plane slowly descending into the
city. "I didn't think planes landed this late," I
said, but Sally was already in the bathroom.

After a while, I found myself thinking
about my older brother, Jake, how he had
gotten off to such a promising start: a good
student, a teacher's favourite, a hit with girls,
captain of the track and field team—even had
his picture in the newspaper one spring day
under the caption, JAKE GILLINGS CHAMPION
PROSPECT! There he was in his whites with a
trophy gleaming in the late afternoon sun.

Champion prospect indeed. I had so admired
him! Watching him on the football field—his
hands on his hips, watching the players move
and shift just before the snap, reading the
play—or making his way down the school
corridor with a cluster of A-list friends, their

jackets open, ties loosened, I felt as though
I was observing a more successful model of
myself. Better-looking (he looked like Kris
Kristofferson), a better soccer player, better at
backgammon, better at water skiing, better at
Ping-Pong, even a better dancer at parties. Just
better, better, better. And believe it or not, I
basked in it. It gave me a charge, as they used to
say, to be connected to him, to have people say,
"Oh, that's Jake's little brother."

But something happened to him in university. It was as though someone switched off the
lights in the house and they never came back on:
an unfinished degree, boarding houses, failed
projects, disappointing travels, uneasy girlfriends, Eastern religions, a string of psychia-
trists (who invariably, after three or four months'
treatment, turned into "assholes"). I saw him
once in a restaurant. He was screaming at a
waitress. I hadn't known he was there until suddenly there was a commotion, smashing plates,

an overturned table, an ashen manager hurrying
across the floor. Where did it come from, this
fury? This capacity to abandon himself to such
a public display of childlike rage? A grown-up
throwing a tantrum. Had some long-haired,
cowboy boot–wearing sixties psychiatrist coun-
selled him to "get in touch with his anger"? And
poor Jake had got it wrong?

Why had he turned on me, who adored him?
Why had he fucked my German girlfriend in my
bed and made sure I heard about it? Why does
he still, according to my cousin, rant at the drop
of a hat about our long-dead parents, how they
ruined his life? Can the dead ruin our lives? Can
their talons be *that* long? Don't we win by dint
of just being here?

And why had he turned on *himself* like
that? This peculiar resignation to not being
happy till he was fifty? Tonight, as I'm writing this, I wonder about him: He's out there in
the city somewhere. But doing what? Thinking

what? He must be, I don't know, sixty-three,
sixty-four.

Are you happy yet, Jake? Are you?

One moment we had been such brothers,
dancing side by side to the Zombies' "She's Not
There" with a pair of sisters at a summer dance.
And now this? What happened? Jake and Kyle.
Chloe and I. What the *fuck* happened?

Something else: I noticed that night in the
restaurant that he was dressed identically to
me—black corduroys, brown leather jacket,
crew-neck sweater and white running shoes. So
odd: two aging schoolboys who hadn't spoken
in years wearing the same clothes. That means
something, I know—but what?

Sally emerged from the bathroom and settled
back down in her chair. "What were you thinking about?" she said.

"Jake and Kyle. Kyle and Jake."

She moved her crutches to the side. "You
know what I want? After I'm gone, I want you

to have a little party for me. Not right away. Nothing maudlin. But a birthday party. A party with lots of wine and candles. Martinis, too."

"Sure."

"I want to be in cheerful company and not be alone."

"Okay, then."

"And there's something else."

"Yes?"

"There's a silver canister in my bedroom. On the dresser."

"Yes, I've seen it."

"Do you know what's in it?"

"No."

"Those are Kyle's ashes. I was supposed to do something or other with them, but I couldn't stand any of the ideas. I couldn't stand, to be honest, to be so finally parted from him."

"What would you like me to do?"

"When you leave here, tonight, tomorrow, whenever, I want you to take the ashes with you.

I can't stand the idea of people poking through my affairs, opening the lid, going, 'What's this?,' maybe flushing it down the toilet or packing it up in a cardboard box and sending it to Chloe in California."

Four

Skinny, sharp-chinned Chloe. A dead ringer for Arthur Rimbaud. Dagger tattoo on her arm. Sally's dark eyes. A lanky girl drifting along the sidewalk on a Sunday morning.

I said, "Tell me a little bit about Chloe. How old is she now?"

"Twenty-six."

"And she's in California?"

"She calls it Cali. You know Chloe—she can't leave the English language alone."

"And doing well?"

"So I gather."

"You sound uncertain."

"She's grown rather secretive. With me, anyway."

"Is she single?"

"She has a friend. That's all she'll tell me."

"Who is it?"

"That's what I asked."

"And?"

"She tells me, in the nicest way, that it's none of my beeswax."

"Beeswax. Her expression?"

"Who else?" Sally fell silent for a moment. "They move on, don't they? It's sort of shocking. You always think it must be something you did. Or did too much of."

"I'm not following."

"Well, put it this way." Sally moved her crutch to a more stable upright position. "She was such an easygoing kid, the kind of teenager who hums while she's doing her homework. Tapping her pencil and humming and watching TV all at the same time. Then one day she came home early from high school, drank half a bottle of Marek's vodka, called her English teacher and told him she was dropping out, that she was tired of being a suck and an asshole. Her words. 'A suck and an asshole.'

"Then she put on her pyjamas, got into bed, threw up so violently that she popped a vein in her throat. The sight of blood on the sheets totally unhinged her. She called an ambulance, which carted her off to the hospital on a gurney. Apparently she waved at one of the neighbours on the way out.

"They didn't pump her stomach or anything. They just gave her a stern talking-to and sent her home that evening. I waited a day or so and then, when she was back on her feet, I said, 'What the hell were you thinking, drinking like that? Phoning Mr. Reed.' And she kept saying, over and over, 'I'm so sad. I'm so sad.'

"And I said, 'What are you sad about?'

"She said, 'I can't say. I don't know. I'm just sad.'

"'Is it me? Do I make you sad?'

"'No, no, Mama,' she said, 'don't be silly. You make me happy. This has nothing to do with you.'"

"And you never found out what it was?" I said.

"No, not really. But she was different after that. She changed her mind about going to university here. I said, 'Well, you could stay in residence downtown on the main campus,' but no, no, she wanted to get out of town—get away from *me*, I think. She sent out a raft of applications, all out of city. McGill offered her a scholarship. So off she went. Marek and I packed her into a yellow van with two school friends and watched her drive down the street one late summer day, and that was that. She was gone."

"Was that painful?"

"Yes, at first. Very painful. Surprisingly painful. I sat in the living room with Marek and drank a bottle of vodka and smoked a whole pack of cigarettes. But that's the way it goes:

The healthy ones leave you behind. It's only the sick ones that stay home." Pause. "The truth is, I think she just outgrew her *mother*."

"And you didn't outgrow her?"

"You never do. It's a bit one-sided that way."

"Do you see her? Talk to her?"

"Oh yes, scads. That's not a problem. But she's guarded now. There are certain things I'm just not permitted to ask about. I'm not even sure there's anything *to* know." She carefully lifted her drink and took a sip. "Unless you know something."

"Me?"

"You talk to her a bit. I know that," she said.

"I do. But not much."

"Tell me. I'm hungry for it. I'm hungry for news about her life."

"It'll probably surprise you."

"Tell me, please."

So I fixed myself another drink, a good stiff belt, and told her what I knew. "It must have

been during her second year at McGill. Yes, that
was it. She was doing a degree in Russian litera-
ture and had this giant apartment on rue Sainte-
Famille in the student ghetto. She was the house
social director. Lots of parties. So many, in fact,
that the police were on a first-name basis with
her. But you know Chloe: when she turns it on,
when she gives you that sun lamp smile, she's
irresistible."

"Go on," her mother said. "I'm loving this."
She was watching the movie of her young daughter living out in the world for the first time.

"I had some business in Montreal that
weekend, a misunderstanding with a supplier—I
was in the pharmaceutical supply business back
then. I gave her a call, saying I was going to be
in town, would she be free. I knew better than to
accept an invitation to stay with her. I need eight
hours of sleep and I sensed that I wouldn't get
that. Besides which, one of the girls she shared
a flat with, Miranda Treece, a skinny Texan,

was far too sexy to be around for a whole weekend. I'd met her once in front of the Park Plaza
in Toronto, and the image of her wandering
around the apartment with dirty hair in a ripped
T-shirt and raggedy-ass jeans—well, you know
what I mean. Forget it.

"I took the train from Toronto—it seemed
like a romantic thing to do—and got a room at
the Hôtel Nelligan in the old part of the city.

"Chloe, it turned out, was in love that
semester with the trombone player of a university swing band. She wanted me to go see him
that same night. You heard about this guy?"

"Not the romantic part."

"At nine o'clock, I was sitting in my hotel
room on the rue Saint-Paul, waiting for her to
pick me up. Then it was ten o'clock, then eleven
o'clock, then midnight, at which point, more
pissed off than offended, I took the phone off
the hook, got under one of those fluffy white
French-Canadian duvets and fell asleep.

"Or I must have. Because I remember I had a little dream. I was walking along a quiet street in Amsterdam when a tree cracked and collapsed into the canal near me. Of course, there was no tree—it was the sound of Chloe banging her bony knuckles on my door. It was two o'clock in the morning. I peeked through the peephole. An unblinking eye circled in black makeup peered at me from the other side. The stuff Keith Richards wears."

"Kohl."

"Right. I opened the door and said, 'Chloe, this is a ridiculous hour to turn up.'

"There were four beautiful young women in the hallway. Made-up faces, jangly party dresses, perfume wafting off them. They looked like movie stars."

Sally listened, motionless with attention. "God, she's beautiful, isn't she? Even if you divide it in half because I'm her mother."

I went on. "I suspected they were martini

girls, which are an expensive breed. I was worried about money that year. You may remember our family stockbroker, Clyde Meadows?"

"No, I never got any of that money. But go on, go on."

"Anyway, Clyde Meadows, that poor son of a bitch, shot himself in the wine cellar of his Rosedale mansion. But not before losing almost all of my inheritance. Jake's too."

Sally said, "Was he the guy whose wife disappeared for a few weeks with the Mexican masseur?"

"Same guy. Anyway, I was pretty broke. *Ergo* that stupid job with the pharmacy company. And I knew that by heading out with these four swans, I was tacitly agreeing to pay for everything.

"Still, they were irresistible—their excitement, their beauty, the smell of them. Miranda, my God. She wore a noodle-strapped dress with a feather boa around her neck. I can't remember where the club was, just that the band was in full session when we arrived. They were swinging through a Glenn Miller standard, 'Moonlight Serenade.' It was like stepping into a Woody Allen film.

"Chloe pointed out the trombone player. He was a classic nightmare for a young woman: lush lips, thick hair, rosy cheeks, a savvy, effortless way of holding his horn between riffs. You could see he took it all for granted—his outrageous beauty, the girls lining the front of the stage, the eternity of his youth. He was a star, and I knew he was going to make her suffer."

"And did he?"

"You never heard this?"

"Not a peep. I think by then she thought she'd already told her mother *too* much. As if, by even mentioning it, she might put a jinx on it."

I took a sip of my drink. I was quite drunk. "You have to be old to say that there's a good side to suffering. But there often is."

"How so?"

"Well, I suppose it was because of the trombonist that Chloe and I got to know each other
that winter.

"She phoned me long-distance the following Sunday morning. On the surface, it was a
courtesy call. Thanks for coming out, for giving
everybody such a swell evening. Two hundred
dollars! Jesus. But there was something just a
little bit sour hanging over the conversation, and
I sensed she was in some kind of discomfort. I
hesitated to inquire, though. I generally try to
avoid asking young women about their romantic
woes—the intimacy is somewhat neutering.

"Still, I felt she was on the edge of something, that all she needed was a small, encourag-
ing push and she could get rid of it, like pulling a
splinter out of her finger. And sure enough, after
a while it came out. The three of them—she, the
trombonist and Miranda Treece, the girl with the
feather boa—had shared a taxi home at the end

of the evening at the jazz club. They stopped
first at the trombonist's. He got out. Miranda,
who was sitting in the front seat, got out, Chloe
thought, to change places. She couldn't see
what was happening, but it was taking longer
than it should to just say good night, and a few
moments later Miranda popped that long neck of
hers into the window and said she was going to
hang around for a bit. See you back at the flat.

"So there she was, our little Chloe, in the
back of the taxi all by herself, going home to
nothing on a Saturday night. Just hearing the
story broke my heart. It really did. It reminded
me of my own disappointments. Everyone has
them. You with Terry Blanchard, me with that
German girl in university, now Chloe. In a way,
the specifics never matter, although at the time
they seem to do nothing *but* matter. They seem
so unique in a creative, cruel way. But they're
not, of course. In the end, all romantic com-
plaints come down to the same thing: You want

somebody who doesn't want you. Or doesn't
want you as much as you want them. A million
variations, but always the same wound. And
while Mr. Trombone may have been myopic,
while he may have been headed for a bad end
fifteen years down the road, for the moment the
truth was the truth, which was that he liked the
skinny girl from Texas more.

"That should have been punishment enough
in itself. But life can be imaginatively spiteful—
it's almost enough to make you believe in a
malevolent deity—so not only did Chloe have to
observe in the brown eyes of the young musician
his waning interest in her, but she was forced
to listen to the nightly shrieks of pleasure from
Miranda Treece's bedroom, which sounded,
according to Chloe, 'like they were murdering
a hog in there!'

"I gave the impotent advice that the non-
involved invariably offer. I suggested that the
next time at bat, she might make herself a little

less available—lay off the phone calls and neighbourly drop-ins. Chloe is an excitable creature, you know that better than I do, and it makes her impatient for things to go her way. I tried to explain to her that Sunday morning that men don't like fish that jump out of the lake into the boat. I was expecting a rewarding burst of laughter. Instead, I encountered granite silence.

"'Chloe, dear,' I said, 'I'm just trying to add some lightness to the situation. It's not life or death.'

"'It is to me,' she said softly."

"Did she say that?" her mother asked.

"Yes, but hang on, hang on. The story isn't finished yet."

I got up and poured myself a glass of water and plopped a handful of ice into it. I could feel a tiny hammer tapping against my right temple, with worse things to come. I even contemplated keeping back one of Sally's sleeping pills for the brutal hangover that was coming up behind me like a silent train.

I sat back down. "I confess, I could feel my heart constrict for Chloe, for the agony she was suffering, and for its probable outcome, which was that things would go on for a while, this nightly scorching, but then, like all unrequited passions in the body of a healthy soul—and Chloe is, if nothing else, a robust soul—it would fizzle and fizzle and fizzle into a state of bemused bewilderment. A state of *What was I thinking?* But it would take a while. The clocks slow down for the heartbroken. It's like watering your fingernails: they grow at the pace they grow and not a second faster."

"Did you say that to her?"

"Yes, but it's like that conversation you had with your mother in the car about Terry Blanchard. It made Chloe feel better for a bit. She even hooted with laughter now and again about the whole situation. But I knew that after

she put down the phone, she was going back to
feeling shitty.

"Sometimes on those nights, when I forgot
to click off the ringer, my phone rang at three
o'clock in the morning. 'Uncle M.?' a young girl's
voice said. But I was happy to hear her voice.
Even if it was just to tell me that the trombonist smelt like bananas if you stood close to him,
or the latest stupid thing Miranda said. But it
was a lonely time in my life. I was single again,
my American girlfriend having returned to her
Arkansas roots, and I was beginning to find it
tiresome to make new friends. Too much work, all
that—the dinners, the conversation, the old stories trotted out once again. Like going to the gym.

"I spent my days on the back roads of
Ontario delivering newfangled toilet seats,
compression stockings, ankle stabilizers, blood
pressure units, walkers—with and without
wheels—to small-town drugstores. It didn't
last long, this season in hell, but it's always

seemed like a failure of nerve on my part to have embraced such a ludicrously unsuitable activity even in a moment of financial panic."

"Surely you don't still see it that way? It sounds rather admirable to me," Sally interrupted.

"What's admirable about it?"

"Just doing it. Just getting up and doing it and not whining about it."

"I whined plenty, don't worry about that. But anyway. To snatch up the phone and hear Chloe's voice, the vibrating aliveness that I had felt so vividly that night in the hotel lobby, made me feel as if I were not standing at the *side* of life, but that I was engaged, however vaguely, at the heart of it.

"She got over the trombone player, and over the next while there was a string of cheerful melodramas, other boys with other trombones. I say cheerful because even while Chloe complained about this boy's cockiness or that boy's insensitivity or this guy's tiresome addictions,

there was a quickness to laughter, an easy teas-
ability. 'Uncle M.,' she'd protest, '*je vous en prie!*
You must desist!' Which meant, Give me more,
give me more. She loved the attention, I think.
In the darkness of my bedroom, I imagined her
raising her face to the ceiling with uncontainable
laughter, as though she were expelling a lungful
of smoke.

"Privately, to be candid, I sympathized with
these young men as they politely eyed the exit
sign. How exhausting Chloe could be, this high-
voltage *being*! It was as if she was born without a
middle gear. Either asleep or hysterical."

Sally laughed, and then I did too.

"'Perhaps,' I said to her one evening on
the phone, 'you should try for older men.' I
was thinking of someone like the French actor
Gérard Depardieu. Do you know him?"

"Yes, yes. Divine."

"A large, big-boned man whose physical and
emotional weight might give our little humming-

bird the perch she required." (I also—and this I didn't mention to my sister—had a mild fever for Chloe myself, and had awoken on a few mornings entertaining fantasies that don't need to be described and certainly didn't need to be acted upon. Besides which, I believed then that Chloe's orientation was toward tall, pretty boys of ambivalent sexual orientation. You like what you like, and there's the end of it.)

"'Maybe you should lay off the gays,' I said on a different occasion. (I'd been drinking.) My suggestion produced a pleased chirp in which I detected a hint of gratitude. Maybe it let her off the hook. It's one thing to get dumped by a lush-lipped young man with a trombone, but quite another for a homosexual to take a pass on you.

"'Okay, Uncle M.,' she said, 'no more fags, I promise.' And again hooted a cloud of invisible smoke at the ceiling.

"I didn't hear back from her. Maybe she got what she needed from me and moved on, I

don't know. But I spotted her on the sidewalk in
Toronto a year or so later. It was Thanksgiving,
a cheerless, Herman Melville kind of day. She
was home for the long weekend. I pulled my
bicycle over to the curb. Her face lit up. She was
on her way to a dress sale at Holt Renfrew at
that very moment. A large shopping bag dangled
from her wrist. She'd already been at it for a
while. Shopping, I mean.

"I noticed, though, that the rouge on her
cheekbones was uneven, the small pink circles
didn't quite match one another. Perhaps she'd
been in a hurry when she left your apartment
that morning and had done a rush job. But there
was something about the way she looked, this
hastily applied rouge, that made me sad. Maybe
it was the fall day—fall has always been a time
of haunting nostalgia for me. Perhaps I was
projecting my own disappointments onto her.
But I don't think so. It was, I think, the image of
this young woman out shopping, as if her young

body was somehow misspent on this activity. That instead of lingering on a dull morning on the sidewalk with a shopping bag, her young body should have been instead lying in the shadows of a bedroom, the curtains stirring, the warmth of a lover's body only inches away. Such a waste, her capacity to love and to *be* loved and no one to share it with.

"But wait. Wait. Things changed."

❧

It was after midnight now. I poured us another round of Drambuie. Sally and I in her eighteenth-floor apartment.

"Damn," she said, "I have to go to the washroom again. Will you hand me my crutches?"

I helped her to her feet. She turned a pale face toward me. "This is all getting less and less manageable." I helped her into the bathroom. There were all sorts of things in there that you

don't see in a regular bathroom. And a chemical
smell that didn't smell human. Like embalming
fluid. And it struck me for a second that that's
how she felt, embalmed. And that this too, and
the things that came with it, she'd had enough
of. I wondered, too, who had phoned, whether I
should have answered it. You never know. But to
go against her wishes had seemed like a violation
of our deal, of my promise.

But while I waited for her to emerge, I found
myself pondering those words, "All this has
become less and less manageable." It was the
second time she'd used those same words, and
I found myself remembering an episode that
had happened only a few months earlier. I had
dropped by her apartment unexpectedly late one
afternoon, the winter night already collecting
like soot between the neighbouring high-rises
and the discarded Christmas trees up and down
the length of the street. It was the final hours of
a sullen January day in Toronto, when even the

cheeriest souls find themselves fingering a length
of rope and looking appreciatively upwards at
the available roof beams. (I'm phrase-making
here, but you know what I mean.)

I buzzed her number. The glass door clicked
open. I went up the elevator and down the hallway, which smelt, as always, of fragrant spices
and large families. Behind one door, a shrill
woman's voice chanted to a stringed instrument
as though she were in mourning for the recently
dead. Behind other doors, animated voices rose
and fell.

Sally was wearing that green dress; her eyes
carefully made up, cheeks lightly rouged, mod-
est lipstick. She stood in the centre of the room,
wobbling slightly on her crutches. It was clear
that she was going out.

"I'm going to see——" She named a Christian
revivalist, a perpetually tanned preacher whose
unconvincing heterosexuality and next-world
promises I had watched off and on for years on

television on those afternoons when a nicotine-
and-bourbon hangover made an excursion out-
doors something you put off until nightfall.

It puzzled me, her going to a revival meeting. What on earth was she thinking? Or *was*
she thinking? Sally was a rigorously intelligent
woman, a bemused and articulate observer of
the world, and for her to embrace the word of a
bullshitter in an ice cream suit seemed tragic.

What was she after, taking an expensive taxi
downtown to Maple Leaf Gardens, sitting in
the front row in a gleaming line of wheelchairs
and crutches, paralyzed limbs and distorted
smiles? Did it mean that my sister had arrived
at such a point of desperation, such a degree
of unhappiness that, like Pascal's gamble about
the existence of God, she had put her common
sense on hold to embrace the possibility that
this mincing Southern millionaire could lay
his hands upon her useless legs and make
them work?

I didn't ask. I was afraid, I suppose, of the
answer. (How ungenerous I was in those days.)
I simply took her down in the elevator and
put her in the back of a taxi and waved as the
red tail lights disappeared in the early evening
darkness.

Over the months, my thoughts sometimes
returned to that revival meeting, to her standing in the middle of the room in her green dress
and glancing away, ever so slightly, when she
told me where she was going. I never thought
of it, never, without a kind of sinking feeling.
But recently I've undergone a change of mind.
Of heart, perhaps. I now see that evening, her
descent into the throng of wounded and broken
and famished souls, as something different, as
something deeply poignant: her gameness, her
willingness to try, even with a smile, *anything*,
for a last kick at everyday happiness. When I
think of my cherished Sally, I always come back
to this word: *heroic*.

(Do the dead forgive us, I wonder?)

The toilet flushed; the bathroom door opened. Sally emerged. She had clearly been thinking about something in there. She said, "Do you remember that television show Chloe worked on?"

"The imitation American police drama."

"Yes, that's the one."

"Sure, I remember. Chloe thought it might be a way into the world of scriptwriting. 'Remunerative but sterile,' I told her that."

"But it looked so promising there for a while. One minute she was bouncy, the next minute she was talking about leaving town."

"You don't know about this?"

"Don't be coy. Tell me."

"Well," I said, a little archly, "I'll put it this way: instead of writing dialogue like 'Step *away* from the vehicle' or 'So what did the lab say?' she ended up in bed with the director. He was married, naturally, a strutting little wizard who could have been a Martin Scorsese or a Tarantino—he had a terrific eye—but he simply couldn't control his appetites for booze and cocaine and pretty assistants with clipboards, and ended up a big-shot director in the wastelands of Canadian dramatic television. And that *is* a tragedy. Jumping into bed with him wasn't."

"You know him?" she said.

"Casually. But I like him. He's a mess, but a gifted mess. Anyway, what Chloe misunderstood from the outset was that she wasn't in university anymore, that in the grown-up world, when you sleep with a woman's husband, particularly a woman who has just had a *baby*, the consequences are—well—different. This wasn't a replay of Miranda and the trombonist. A few weeks into the first season, the director's wife got wind of things. She turned up at Chloe's apartment. She put a Japanese carving knife to her *own* throat and said that if she, Chloe, didn't

stop fucking her husband, she (the wife) would
slit herself from ear to ear.

"The drama played itself out over the next
few months: bursts of hysteria, sulks, alcoholic
confessions, blistering hangovers and public
scenes, until the director did what he was
destined to do all along, which was to return,
droop-tailed, to his wife and work a solid, if
brief, program at the Hillside rehab centre
in Georgia. Eight thousand dollars a week.
Nevertheless, a month later he was slugging
back shot glasses of Russian vodka and got
himself arrested for, get this, trying to strangle
his wife outside a Yorkville restaurant.

"Never mind what addiction counsellors
say, the only way to get over the loss of a cherished lover is to find a body that thrills you as
much as the one you've lost. I know this from
personal experience. (And not just once, either.)
But when you're young, you think getting
out of town will do the trick, and that's what

Chloe decided to do. She thought about going to law school, somewhere 'cool'—Mexico, the Caribbean maybe. She fancied herself a criminal lawyer, getting those Puerto Rican and Jamaican drug dealers a day in the sunshine of level-field jurisprudence. But after spending four or five days in the gallery at the University Avenue courthouse, she came to the conclusion that pretty much everyone down there is guilty. But worse, from her standpoint, was the daily spectacle of the doors of justice spinning like some nightmare fan, coughing out the same burnt-out lawyers and the same felons week in and week out. She said to me on the phone one day, 'I get the distinct feeling that the best part of being a lawyer is going to law school. After that, it's strictly downhill.' My guess is that she was probably right, and I told her so. But considering what I was doing for a living at the time, I'm not so sure it was prudent advice."

"And that got her to California?"

"Here's where the story gets good. After the
TV show, she pissed around here and there. She
wrote half a novel about a young girl who falls
in love with a married film director. But the truth
is, Chloe never had much affection for her own
company, or for sitting in a room with her own
shortcomings (who does?), so she gave it up. For
a few months she taught English to Cambodian
refugees in Vancouver, then did a night shift
on a suicide hotline. Then worked for an essay
writing service. Then painted sets for the low-
budget horror film *Santa Claws*. Nothing quite
worked. She phoned me one night, she was a bit
drunk, said she was on her way back to Toronto,
that she wanted to help the 'little brown babies in
India.' She meant it, too. But she never went."

"Yes," Sally said, "I recall that stage. The
little brown babies stage."

"One day, while she was working in a book-
store, she happened across a copy of *Vanity
Fair*. On the cover was a photograph of the

magazine's staff, mostly young people, sitting on desks, talking on the phone. She faxed it to me. That's what I want to do, she wrote—I want to do something with *people*. And that was it: a year later she was in California doing a very expensive degree in journalism."

"But where did the *money* come from? Not from me. And certainly not from her father," Sally said.

"How she got there, that was vintage Chloe. Other people could have done it, but few with the same panache. She called it her SP. Her Secret Project. When I inquired, she clammed up, got very mysterious. Until, that is, she sensed I was getting pissed off—I don't especially care for protracted intrigue—and confessed. Get this. She wrote a letter to the fifteen richest people in Canada and asked them to sponsor her degree. 'I'm Chloe Sanders,' her letter declared, 'and I'd like to do a master's degree at UC Berkeley in California. The tuition is forty thousand dollars

a year. In exchange for your support, I will write
you one letter a month with the details of my life
on the West Coast.'

"It was an absurd proposition, but I loathe
dream squashers, so I kept my mouth shut.
Fourteen millionaires returned their regrets, but
one guy, the retired owner of a string of mul-
tinational copper mines, nibbled. Could he see
her letter of acceptance? She mailed it to him.
A week later, she got the following telegram:
'Pack your bags, Chloe Sanders, you're going to
Berkeley.'"

"In exchange for what?"

"That's exactly what I said. But it turned
out, in exchange for nothing. In fact, the guy
wrote the cheques on his *wife's* account." I went
on: "I've often wondered about that gesture, her
writing strangers and asking for money with the
assurance of an adored child. Where did she get
the outrageous confidence? And it occurs to me,
and not without a certain envy, that the answer

lies in the question. She *was* an adored child.
And that's you, Sally. That's you."

We both sat silently for a while. Then Sally
said, "I'm not making excuses for Chloe, for
her cutting me out of whole sections of her
life, but she had to do a lot of things that most
young girls don't, things that they usually have
done *for* them. She had to learn to shop for gro-
ceries, to buy brown bread and not white bread,
to buy healthy morning cereal, not the sug-
ary junk her friends ate; how to detect a fresh
cantaloupe; how to separate the whites from the
darks downstairs in the laundry room; how to
make scrambled eggs (no milk at a low heat).
How to drive a car in the winter (turn *into* the
skid). She had to learn not to forget her lunch,
because she had a mother who couldn't pop by
the school and drop it off. All that must have
been a hardship."

"Perhaps," I agreed, "but it made her excep-
tionally *able*."

"Almost frighteningly able. But go on, please."

"It must have been a lonely time, those first few months in an American city. Setting up a little apartment, eating dinner alone. Trying to make friends without seeming too hungry for friends. She started to phone me again. Chloe only phones me when she's bleak. But that's fine. She joined a 'Newcomers to Berkeley' society; she even went to church a few times. She went to Alcoholics Anonymous, not because she had a drinking problem but because there were people there. Because they all went out for coffee after the meeting and everyone was welcome.

"And then, one rainy November night, a young woman stepped out of the rain, folded up her umbrella and joined the circle of chairs. It was Miranda Treece, her old nemesis from Montreal. And she *did* have a drinking problem. She had done very little with her life in the inter-vening years except live on her family's money and fuck a whole bunch of guys. She'd washed up in Berkeley on the heels of a failed romance and didn't have the steam to leave town. I don't know the details or even the timing, but one day Chloe found a small parcel in her mailbox. She opened it up. It was a T-shirt. And with it was a short handwritten note: *I wore this for three days. If you like how it smells, call me.* It was signed *Miranda*. And that, as they say, was that."

I looked over at Sally. She was frowning as if she had not heard me correctly. But I wanted her to hear the end of the story before she responded. "Chloe has always been strangely private about that chapter of her life, even with me. Which is funny, because she could be alarmingly candid about her goings-on with men. Not with this, though. But when I saw her coming out of a movie theatre in Toronto with Miranda one afternoon a year or two later, there was a bloom on her cheeks, those lovely cheeks that had made me so sad that Sunday afternoon

on the sidewalk. It was the kind of illumination
that even a fool can see comes from being physi-
cally loved."

I stopped talking. We both watched the
candle flame for a while. Another plane, its tail
illuminated like that of a bright red goldfish,
descended over the airport. The events that
happened in the wake of this conversation still
seem extraordinary to me, the way life does
and doesn't work out. And for whom. But
here's something that *did* work out. Let's jump
ahead eight or nine years after that evening on
the eighteenth floor. Chloe and Miranda came
over to my apartment for dinner with their two
children in tow (gay dads, turkey baster, enough
said). Watching them from where I sat at the end
of the table, I couldn't help reflecting on how
delicious, how mysterious it was that Miranda,
this great love of Chloe's life, now her legal
wife, was the same girl who had once routed her
for a boy who currently, I'm told, delivers booze

in a little green car for an after-hours supplier. Near the end of the night, Miranda did a perfect handstand in the kitchen. The children were beside themselves with wonder. It turned out she'd been the San Antonio gymnastics champion during her last year of high school.

Five

IT WAS NEARLY THREE IN THE MORNING NOW.
The hum from the refrigerator clicked off,
leaving the room in audible silence. It seemed
as though the curtains, the lamps, the pictures
on the wall were all waiting too. I was standing at the window looking down at the parking
lot. A man in a white jacket moved between the
cars and stepped under a spotlight. He looked
up. We looked at each other for an unnaturally
long time. Then he waved, a big wide wave as
though he were on a boat and trying to catch
the attention of a passing freighter. But I didn't
wave back. He seemed like bad luck and I
stepped away from the window.

Sally came out of the bathroom and sat

down heavily on the indentation on the couch, her usual place, and put her crutches carefully to one side, held them in place for a moment to be sure they didn't wobble over. "I'm ready to do this thing now," she said.

I looked at her face. It was grey and a little puffy, the face of an exhausted person, a party-goer who has come to the end of the night, knows it, but is too exhausted, among the wilting flowers and sweating cheese and lipstick-stained wineglasses, to get up and make it across the room to the door. Too tired to enjoy staying, too tired to leave.

I leaned forward in my chair. I closed my fingers together and then stretched them out. I saw she was watching my fingers. Then she looked up at me with a soft smile. "Could we skip this next part?"

I knew what she meant, of course, but I needed to hear her say it. "Which part would that be?"

"The questions that have obviously occurred to me a thousand times."

"And tonight's the night?"

"If you love me, please don't make me plead."

"Okay."

"Do you have them?"

"Yes."

"Are they with you?"

I took the dark bottle from my shoulder bag, which I had laid on the floor beside my chair.

"Are there enough?"

"Yes, Sally, there are enough."

"I don't have to take, like, two *hundred* of them, do I?"

"No."

"How many do I have to take?"

"Thirty. Tops."

She looked at the bottle. "It looks scary, that bottle. Can't we put them in something else?"

I got up, went into the kitchen, opened the pill bottle, removed the cotton batten (we didn't need a sinister rattle coming from my bag as I crossed the room).

The phone rang again.

"Who the hell *is* that?" she said.

"Should I get it?"

"God, no. Please don't. Let's get on with this." After a moment, she said, "I don't want to throw up, be found half alive in a pool of vomit and spend the rest of my days with the IQ of a cabbage."

"You know, Sally, for someone who says she's had enough, you're an awfully amusing woman."

"Death concentrates the mind. I must have read that somewhere."

"No, I believe that's an original."

She thought about it for a second; quietly mouthed the words again. "You're sure? I don't want to go out on a plagiarized note."

"It's yours. Straight up."

"Where were we?" she said. I was about to

open my mouth to protest, but she silenced me
with a tilt of her head, a reminder to not make
her plead.

I said, "Let's have a drink first."

"Yes, something fun." (A hint of postpone-
ment?)

"Okay."

"What's fun?"

"Well," I said, "what drink would you order
if we were at the Cucaracha in Mexico?"

"A margarita."

"Have you got the ingredients?"

"I sure as hell do."

"You tell me what to do and I'll do it."

"Hang on," she said, "I'll come into the
kitchen with you."

"Stay where you are."

"I have eternity to sit on my behind. Besides,
there's a stool in there."

So she came into the kitchen with me and
told me how to make a margarita.

And when we were done, we toasted each
other. Then I turned off the light and brought
the drinks back into the living room and sat hers
down by her side.

She said, "Would you get me a glass of
water, please. A big one."

"Cold or warm?"

"Just medium."

I put it beside her margarita. Then I said, "Is
it too late? Can we put some music on?" I found
myself thinking of the man in the white jacket in
the parking lot, waving. "What would you like
to hear?"

"Well," she said thoughtfully, "I'd like to
hear 'Take Five.' You know that one. Dave
Brubeck. I've always loved that drum solo."
(The approach of death, in the same way the
prospect of the day's first drink rejuvenates an
alcoholic, had made her chatty). "It's the only
drum solo I've ever liked."

Or perhaps it was nerves, now that we were
here, finally, at last.

"I agree."

"Normally I hate drum solos," she said.

I clicked through her small CD collection and there it was, the Picasso-like cover. I put it on. We listened to those delicious opening bars, cymbal and crisp snare drum.

"Now listen for the piano, that gorgeous piano," she said. "My grandparents made me take piano for a while. They knew I was artistic, but they just had the wrong thing. But they meant well."

The green liquid in her drink tilted to the rim. She reached into the bowl of pills and took one and then another. It dropped from her hand onto the carpet. I got it for her and put it back in the bowl.

She said, "This song makes me nostalgic for a life I never had. Have you ever had a song that does that to you?"

"Yes," I said, "but with me it's more to do with smells. Pears soap makes me feel like that."

"Isn't that funny. Kyle loved the smell

of Pears soap. I think it evoked a life that he wanted, an organized comfort that he lacked the discipline to create for himself and knew it. Even when he was a little boy, he loved it. What do you make of that?"

"I honestly don't know."

"Do you think he intuited, even then, how things were going to go?"

I shook my head and smiled somewhat foolishly, or so it felt. We listened to the music. The saxophone was fading, making way for the drum solo.

"I don't mean I wish I'd had a different life," she continued. "I had a decent life. I could have done without that fucking carpet, but all in all, lots of love, a wonderful daughter . . ." Her eyes clouded for a moment; she was thinking of Kyle. "But when I hear 'Take Five,' especially the piano (there, you hear it?), I feel like some part of me grew up in Manhattan and went to great parties. For some reason, I always think of

Playboy magazine when I hear this song. Men
with tie pins. Hugh Hefner." She reached into
the bowl and, with some difficulty, removed
two pills.

"I'll get it," I said.

"No, no, I'm fine." She put one pill then the
other in her mouth, threw back her head, her
black hair falling to her shoulders, then straightened up and took a sip of water. "You know,
when I was a little girl, I used to ride cows.
Honest."

I said, "How come you never came to live
with us?"

She thought for a full minute. That's a long
time in real time. I could feel myself sobering
up more quickly than I wanted. Then: "I used
to think that it was because your father didn't
want to raise another man's child. For years I
believed that. But near the end of her life, when
the booze and the pills were starting to make
her a little sloppy with her stories, Mother let

something slip. I understood suddenly that it was her, *she* was the one who didn't want me around."

"Mother? Really?"

"Really."

"Did you see much of her?" I said.

"She'd come and go. When she felt like it. When she felt sentimental."

"But her own daughter, surely—"

"Most of the awful things in life turn out to have quite banal reasons—I've learned that. You know what I think? I think she thought her new man might like her more if she didn't come with so much furniture. It might be even more banal than that. Maybe I was too old; maybe having a daughter my age contradicted something she'd said about her *own* age. Once she got him, got him married, then it was okay to let the cat out of the bag. I remember going on a holiday with her once, one of the few times. I was all grown up and married by then, and determined to get over what a shitty mother she'd been. We went to a beach resort with black sand in Antigua. First night we were in the hotel, just as we were heading downstairs for dinner, she asked me not to tell anyone I was her daughter, to say that I was a cousin."

I said, "Why were you determined not to hate her? Why do you have to love everyone in your family just because they're family?"

"I can see you're thinking of your brother, Jake, again."

"He's just an example."

She said, "The truth is, sometimes I really loved my mother. When I was a little girl, I used to daydream about falling asleep in her arms. And then she'd turn up at my grandparents' and be funny and worldly and hug me and tell me I was beautiful and we'd go for these drives and I'd forgive her all over again."

"And then?"

"And then she'd go away again. Sometimes

it looked like she wanted to be sure she still had me. Then she was free to get on with her life, knowing I was still there."

"But you forgave her in the end."

"Just before she died, yes, I did."

"Did she know that?"

"Yes, yes. She let her guard down once. And I got to say everything I needed to say."

"And what'd she say?"

"She just listened. That's what I needed her to do. Just listen and not argue; not defend herself; not go on the attack. And then she said, 'You're right.' And then we were okay. I never quite trusted she wouldn't take off on me— people who do that seldom do it just once—but still, we had some fun. I just kept her a little distant from my heart."

Sally took another four or five pills and threw her head back and swallowed. "Besides, at some point it seems like we all leave someone we love by the side of the road and drive away. I did it to Kyle when I put him on that bus in Mexico; she did it to me to get a new husband."

And I did it to you, I thought. I sat up. "It sounds rather grand, but I'm going to say it anyway. All sins are not equal. Putting a self-destructive teenager on a bus is not the same as leaving your daughter to grow up elsewhere. It just isn't."

Or not bothering to visit your crippled sister.

The drum solo from "Take Five" concluded and, like a slippered guest entering a room, the saxophone resumed.

"Anyway," she said, and I could see she didn't want a debate. That she had arrived at an understanding from which she did not want to be dislodged.

I said, "And her new husband? What did you think of him?"

"Your father?"

"Yeah."

"Very old school guy. Blazer and these

beautiful starched white shirts and such lovely, lovely cufflinks. He smelt like Old Spice after-shave. Just a hint. We could not have been more different, but we made each other laugh—don't ask me why. I also thought he fancied me a bit. Nothing overt; there was just a little extra spar-kle in the way he talked to me or the very, very gentle way he touched my back when we were going into a room together. I don't think Mother much liked that. But I did. It was an impotent way to level the score, but there you go."

"But nothing more?"

"It crossed my mind, but that would have poisoned my heart as well as hers. No. Mother had her own inferno—you know what your dad was like. He was way out there on the margins. And not just financially. He screwed half her friends, even the unattractive ones. It sounds hos-tile, but it wasn't. It was just greedy. No, in the end our mother didn't get away with anything. No one does. In a way, we all have it coming."

I wanted to keep her talking; she took
such palpable pleasure in conversation, she
danced such an elegant dance when she spoke,
that I thought for a second it might occur to her
to stay around and do some more. I also knew
that if things went as planned, these were the
final chapters, the final paragraphs, the final
sentences I would ever get from her. From
some point not so far down the road, there
would be a clean line, an end, and from there I
would have only past conversations to revisit;
and they, like the paint on an old house, would
fade gently away. And I would partially forget
them and then people would forget me and then
there'd be nothing left of us or this evening.

"So you grew up with your grandparents. In
the country. And that was——?"

"You want to keep me talking," she said with
a smile. "And I'm happy to. Just please don't
confuse it for something else. Okay?"

"Okay."

"Promise?"

I nodded.

"We were seven miles out of town, the nearest neighbour was a farmer across a cornfield. The school bus came to the top of the driveway every morning. It was all fine. Until puberty. Then living in the country's not so good. It always feels like you're missing something. And you are, in fact. Then one day a car rolled up the driveway and Bruce Sanders got out. And that was that."

She took three pills and swallowed them. Both of us, Sally and I, retreated into private thought. Surfacing, I said, "What are you thinking about?"

She jerked as if she had been suddenly startled. "Something ridiculous."

"Tell me."

"It's not the sort of thing you're supposed to be thinking about at times like this." Turning a frowning, half-smiling face toward me, she said,

"Do you ever have a song in your head that you can't get rid of?"

"Yes. Do you?"

"Yes."

"What is it?"

"It's the theme song from that television show, *The Waltons*."

"Right. I remember that show."

"I always liked that man, the actor who played John-Boy's father. Do you know his name?"

"No. But I remember the theme song."

"Now we're *both* hearing it," she said with a dry smile that made my heart contract.

More pills. I could hear her fingernails rattle against the side of the glass bowl.

The music changed. Glenn Miller's "Moonlight Serenade." I hadn't heard it since that night with Chloe in the Montreal jazz club.

"Nice song," I said.

She looked up sleepily. "Glenn Miller, Tommy Dorsey, Benny Goodman. One of those guys. I can't remember."

We listened, both of us, those easygoing saxophones floating overhead like clouds.

"I have another favour to ask," she said. "I want you to tell Chloe about this night we had. I want you to do it soon. I don't want her to think I died sad and alone. Will you do that?"

"I will."

"Do you promise? Look me in the eye and promise."

And I did. And I suddenly realized who the caller on the phone was.

She sighed. "Will you dance with me? I want to remember what it's like to be held in a man's arms."

So we danced, the two of us. She dropped her crutches and I carried her, my chin to hers, and it struck me the way she nestled her chin into my shoulder that she was, after all this, still very much a girl at a teenage dance.

"Do you think there's an afterlife?" she said.

She was sinking into sleep. I said, holding her tight, holding her for my own life, it seemed, "If there *is*, will you let me know?"

A slow sigh, her eyes closed. "How would I do that?"

"Find a way to let me know. Find a way to tell me."

For a second, I thought she had fallen asleep, but then her hand stirred and she said, "What would you do then?"

"I don't know. Maybe behave better. Or worse."

"It's best not to know."

"But don't you want to know?" I said.

Another sleepy pause, her head dropping down near her chest.

"I think I'd like to lie down. Will you help me?"

She was dead weight, her head bobbing against my shoulder. I lifted her in my arms and I took her and laid her on the couch on her back and straightened her legs and put a pillow under her head and sat beside her. I took her hand. It was still so warm, so lifelike. Her pulse fluttered like a tiny bird under her skin.

"When I was a little girl," she said, "I used to go to sleep on the porch during the summer. They had a little bed out there for me. And sometimes, in the middle of the night, it'd start to rain. How I *loved* the sound of that rain. My grandfather used to come out, and he'd say, 'Sally, do you want to come inside?' And I'd say, 'No, Grandpa, I want to lie here. Will you stay with me?' And he'd say yes and sit down, and I could hear him settle into the chair and light his pipe, and I could smell the smoke drifting over to me, this delicious blue smoke, and I was so, so, so happy—just the rain and my warm bed and my grandfather's tobacco. I was happy for eternity."

"I'll stay with you," I said.

"Will you?"

"Yes, Sally, yes, I will stay with you."

For a long time, nothing, and then she mumbled something. I leaned over. "What?" I whispered. I put my ear to her mouth. "Yes?"

And then she said, or I think she said, "I'm almost there."

Some quarter of an hour later, she took a deep breath, as though she was going to say something; and then she slowly exhaled. And then I never heard her breathe again. I kissed her on the forehead. I could feel the life leaving her body. I said, "I love you, I love you. Please take this with you wherever you're going."

I had never before sat in the room with death. But I stayed with her because I have always suspected that there is something between dying and dying, a zone of after death that precedes extinction. And I wanted her to have company for it. Who knows when we're

really born into consciousness or when we
leave it?

I remained in my chair, holding her hand,
speaking quietly to her. Suddenly, a wave of
goosebumps covered my whole body; my voice
broke; the tears streamed down my cheeks. "I'm
so sorry," I said. "I'm so sorry."

Her hand grew still colder, and as it grew
colder, I could feel a change come over her, *see* a
change rather, and I understood for the first time
in my life that we are born with a soul and that it
inhabits our body our whole lifetime and when we
die, reluctantly, like children leaving a park, our
soul very gently disengages and moves off, like
a shadow, and takes with it all that ever made us
human, all that ever made us *us*. And behind, in
its wake, is just a body, an uninhabited residence.
The doors blowing open, the windows creaking.
Grass growing up in the cracks in the floor.

So this is death, I thought. I touched my
sister's face. It too had grown cold.

But still I stayed. "Will you tell me?" I said. "Will you find a way to tell me?" But from this body on the chesterfield in front of me, in its green dressing gown, her lips lipsticked, her brow unwrinkled, I knew that she had gone, and it felt as if I was talking to no one, talking to an empty room.

"Where did you go?" I said. "Where are you now?"

But there was no answer.

"Is there anyone there with you?"

I stayed with Sally's body until the sun came all the way up, a morning, I recall, almost metallic in its sheen. I taped the note about calling the police to the outside of her door. Then, certain the hall was empty, with the ashes of her son under my arm and my bottle of pills rattling like teeth in my pocket, I kissed her on the forehead. "Goodbye, Sally," I said, "goodbye," and then I went down the back stairs and went home.